From the library of

SOPHENE

HOVHANNES TOUMANIAN

DAVID OF SASSOON

TRANSLATED BY

THOMAS SAMUELIAN

SOPHENE BOOKS

Los Angeles

Published by Sophene 2022

David of Sassoon («Սասունցի Դաւիթը») was first published by Hovhannes Toumanian in 1903. The Armenian text in this edition is reproduced from Toumanian's anthology (Constantinople, 1922).

First translated into English by Thomas Samuelian in 1997.

A searchable, digital copy of this book can be accessed at:
https://arak29.org/david-of-sassoon

www.sophenebooks.com
www.sophenearmenianlibrary.com

ISBN-13: 978-1-925937-94-7

INTRODUCTION

David of Sassoon

The name "David" comes from the Hebrew for "the beloved one." Like the Old Testament David who slew Goliath, David of Sassoon is the beloved, national hero, the defiant and self-reliant youth, who by the grace of God defends his homeland in an unequal duel against a titanic oppressor.

The *David of Sassoon* presented here is Hovhannes Toumanian's captivating rhymed version of the third cycle of the epic. The epic spans four generations of the house of Sassoon, a mountainous enclave of the Armenian highlands, west of Lake Van and Mt. Ararat, known for its hearty folk and indomitable spirit. The epic took shape in the 10th century based on an oral tradition spanning centuries. The earliest written reports of the epic were made by Portuguese travelers in the 16th century. The basic text of the epic was first recorded in 1873 by Fr. G. Srvandzdyants. The full epic is a hefty tome that, one can imagine, took medieval tellers days to recite, easing the boredom of the long, lonely winters for these highland shepherds.

The epic begins with two brothers, Sanasar and Balthasar. Some scholars link them to the brothers Adramelek and Sarasar, the sons of Hezekiah,[1] the king of Israel during the siege of Jerusalem by Sennacherib, King of Assyria. Movses Khorenatsi, the father of Armenian history, considered the Artsruni dynasty of Armenia, which ruled in and around Vaspurakan[2] and reached its height from 908 to 1021, to be descended from Sanasar.[3] According to Armenian tradition, the two sons settled near the mountain called Sim, which some have identified as a mountain in Sassoon. The pair of brothers resurface in the Armenian epic as the immaculately conceived sons

---

1   2 Kings 19:37, Isaiah 37:38.
2   The region from Lake Van to Lake Urmia.
3   Movses Khorenatsi's *History of the Armenians*, II.5,7, III.55.

of the Armenian princess Dzovinar, who was taken from Armenia to Baghdad by the Caliph when most of Armenia was under Arab domination.[4] The Caliph decides to kill them, but before he can, they escape to Armenia. After slaying dragons, building cities, and restoring Armenia to prosperity, the brothers return to Baghdad to rescue their mother.

In the epic of David of Sassoon, the Moslems (referred to as Musr or Egypt in this version of the epic) and their leader (referred to as Melik)[5] may have displaced the Assyrians, and two thousand years of history may be compressed into a single storyline, but the north-south geopolitical dynamic between Armenia and Mesopotamia persisted in the people's collective memory and remained deeprooted in the repertoire of Armenian oral tradition.

The next cycle is the story of David's father, Lion Mher, who is the epitome of the noble, wise, fair and self-sacrificing father-king. Approaching old age without an heir, he accepts with gentility the passing of his generation as the price of the next generation. As the reading from the Armenian requiem states, "except a grain of wheat falls into the earth and dies, it remains alone; but if it dies, it bears fruit".[6] Lion Mher represents the strength of nature and rectitude of character that bears fruit in his son, David, who is raised an "orphan, no keeper on earth."

David's story resonates not only with the Old Testament David, but also with the battle between Hayk of Armenia and Bel of Assyria. Hayk is the Armenian Orion,[7] the deified archer-protector-forefather of the Armenians. His deification has been linked by some scholars to the Prometheus story in Greek mythology. In Movses Khorenatsi's history, the story of Hayk's titanic battle with Bel is one of the key episodes in the formation of the Armenian people. Hayk was a handsome, friendly man, with curly hair, sparkling eyes, and strong arms. He was a man of giant stature, a mighty

---

4   7th to 9th centuries.
5   Melik: "king".
6   John 12:24.
7   Job 9:9.

archer and fearless warrior. Hayk and his people, since the time of their forefathers Noah and Japheth lived in and around Mt. Ararat (whence the name of the region below Ararat, Nakhichevan – "the place where Noah descended"). To the south ruled a wicked giant, Bel. Bel tried to impose his tyranny upon Hayk's people. But proud Hayk refused to submit to Bel. After major battles, Hayk delivers his people and restores freedom to his homeland. This north-south struggle is a recurrent theme in Armenian history, repeated in the century from 750 to 850 between the Armenian Bagratuni kingdom of Ani and their Arab overlords. According to some scholars, a century later, David Bagratuni surfaces as David of Sassoon, the fearless, freedom-loving youth, and Hovnan Bagratuni as Uncle Ohan, the cringing appeaser.

An epic cannot be summed up in a single word or from a single point of view. Each reader and listener will relate to certain characters and events in different ways. Nevertheless, the image of David of Sassoon, his nobility, fearlessness, strength, and simplicity, while having special significance for Armenians, has a universal appeal that speaks to all peoples.

Finally, a word about this translation. There are several English translations of *David of Sassoon*, including a blank verse translation of Toumanian's version of this work. So why this translation? Primarily because no other English translation has attempted to replicate the rhymes and rhythms of the Toumanian version, in short, the music of the poetry that draws the reader in and pulls the reader forward through line after line of this marvelous epic work.

Thomas J. Samuelian
Yerevan, August 1999

DAVID OF SASSOON

I

G reat Lion Mher, with his noble pride,
for forty long years ruled Sassoon far and wide.
His rule was so awesome that in his day,
across Sassoon's peaks even birds feared to stray.
Far from the highlands where Sassoon was found,
his dreaded fame spread with a thunderous sound.
And praise for the high deeds of Lion Mher,
on thousands of lips, in one voice, filled the air.

II

He ruled in Sassoon with lionly might,
the prince of the highlands, unchallenged in right.
For forty long years he ruled without foe,
and in forty long years he knew not one woe.
But now as old age upon him descended,
this valiant man's heart a pang apprehended,
which prompted the aging grand hero to ponder:
"My life's autumn days will soon take me yonder,
the captive of earth and its black sandy cloak.
The fame of Mher shall vanish like smoke,
and my name, and my might, and my glory shall pass,
in my orphaned and leaderless realm shall amass
thousands of bandits and fiends on the make,
no heir have I left, no successor to take
my sword in his hand for Sassoon's protection,"
so thought the great prince in pensive dejection.

III

Then one day, as he thought, his grey eyebrows knit tight,
an angel from heaven, in fiery light,
came to the prince, feet fixed on a cloud,
bringing a message, proclaiming aloud:

"Greetings! your highness, O Sassoon's great lord,
your voice to God's throne in high heaven has soared,
and soon shall he grant you the heir that you seek.
Heed me well, though, prince Mher, great king of this peak,
on the day that the Lord gives effect to your prayer,
neither you nor your wife shall he suffer to spare."

"May God's will be done," said Mher without sigh,
"Death is our lot; all mortals must die.
But when in this world we've a child in our stead,
through our child we live, although we be dead."

And then in a flash, the Angel took flight,
and nine months and nine hours from that joyous sight,
to Lion Mher a child was born,
and he called his cub David. On that happy morn,
he summoned his brother Ohan of Great Voice,
and his realm he bequeathed, no time to rejoice,
to his brother Ohan and his newly born son,
knowing his days and his wife's were now done.

IV

In those times, reigned a king, over Egypt victorious,
called Melik of Musr, mighty and glorious.
As soon as he learned of Great Mher's demise,
he set for Sassoon to conquer a prize.
Ohan of Great Voice trembled in fear,
bowing his head, as the warlord came near.
Down on his knees, begging he said,

"You be our master," quaked he with dread,
"So long as we're under the force of your sway.
We'll be your true servants, your tribute we'll pay.
But on one condition, our land must remain,
untouched and intact for as long as you reign."

"No," said Melik, "your whole nation must go,
under my sword their submission to show,
and prove that whatever my policy be,
no native of Sassoon shall rise against me."

Ohan called his people from near and from far.
They passed one by one 'neath Melik's scimitar.
All except David, who try though they did,
refused to do honor as Melik had bid.
The crowd dragged him forward by force to his foe.
Raging, he tossed them away, high and low.
He grazed his small finger against a large rock,
emitting a lightning bolt to the crowd's shock.

"This rogue, he is trouble, I must kill him off,"
said the King to the elders, who started to scoff.

"King," they protested, "you're mighty and strong.
How could this young lad do you any wrong,
though he were fire from head down to foot,
after everyone under your sword you have put?"

"You think you know best," said Melik, with alarm.
"But be warned, if upon me should ever come harm,
upon this boy's head shall the penalty rest,
as this day's defiant events do attest."

V

At the time of this clash, David the great,
was but a small boy, of seven or eight.
A boy though I say, he was strong as could be.
All were the same to him, man, beast or flea.
It's an old saying, but truth it does hold,
"Eat up your porridge, grow up strong and bold."
But pity this child, no keeper on earth,
although Mher's son, they knew not his worth.

Ohan of Great Voice had a mean, wicked wife.
Her tongue she first held, then started the strife:

"I'm only one person, with thousands of cares,
enough mouths to feed, without rearing theirs.

What did I do that you took in this knave?
I'm telling you straight, I'm nobody's slave.
I'll bury this boy, if you don't send him packing,
so set something up, work's what he's lacking."

And then she began to moan and complain,
that she was so poor, that all was in vain.
Her burdens were boundless, at least in her eyes:
"I've no keeper, no helper, no pity, no prize."

Ohan went and thought, now what shall I do?
He found iron boots, for the boy as a shoe,
and a large iron rod, to sling on his back.
A shepherd he made him, Sassoon's sheep to track.

VI

Our hero the shepherd tended his sheep.
He wandered the hills of Sassoon high and steep.

Hey, my dear highlands,
O Sassoon's highlands,

He shouted in joy, his voice echoed so,
rumbling it bounced from the peaks high and low.
And the birds and the beasts fled their lairs and their nests,
scampering on rocks, with no where for rest.
David gave chase o'er the hills and the vales,
the fox and the deer, the hares and the quails.

Gathering them up, he climbed top the rocks,
he mixed them all up with the sheep in his flocks.
Down to the town of Sassoon they stampeded,
with noise, dust and uproar, they brayed and they bleated.
The city folk cried, their eyes not believing.
The livestock charged forth, the town's life upheaving.

"Oh help, someone save us!"
The children cried out.
The grown-ups in panic
their work threw about.

Wherever they hid, at home, church or store,
they locked up the windows and bolted the door.
When David arrived and stood in the square,
he looked all about, but no one was there.

"Yo there, he shouted, it's too soon to sleep,
I've come with your goats, and brought you your sheep.
Goatherds and shepherds, get up from the sack,
for each one I took, ten I've brought back.
Hurry, come get them and take them away
to your barns for safekeeping, or else they will stray."

But no one came out, the doors didn't budge.
Back to the hills, too tired to trudge,
he pulled up a rock and rested his head,
and soon fell asleep, the square for a bed.

When the sun rose, the town's folk emerged
at old Ohan's house, they quickly converged.
"Hey there, old Ohan of the Great Voice,
it's you or the kid, you've left us no choice.
How could you put our whole flock in his hands?
The town's filled with beasts, he's ruined our lands.
He can't tell a fox from a lamb. What a mess!
So find him another job, quick, and God Bless!"

VII

Ohan rushed away his nephew to see,
"Uncle, tread softly, these goats like to flee,"
said David, who'd spent all night keeping them there.
But as he approached, the ears of a hare
perked up and he dashed away into the wood,
and David gave chase as fast as he could.
Over the hills and over the dales,
he chased the grey hare through the mountainous trails.
He caught him and brought him right back to the camp,
mixed him in with the goats, and then smiled like a champ.

   "The black ones, God bless them, I like them just fine,
but, Uncle, the grey ones, they won't stay in line.
All day, yesterday, they hopped all around.
In order to catch them, I covered some ground,"

Ohan took a look at David's new boots.
Iron shoes were not equal to David's pursuits.
The rod like the boots was worn away,
so much had he run in only one day.

"David, my lad," he said with affection,
"Those grey ones abused your valiant protection,
I'll leave you no more to their wily devices,
tomorrow, for you cow pasture suffices."

Ohan went his way, and on the next morn,
he brought new steel boots for the ones that were worn,
and a new iron staff for David's strong hand,
and made David guard of Sassoon's pasture land.

VIII

Up to the pasture he went with his herds,
to Sassoon's still highlands, fair beyond words.

O my dear highlands,
Sassoon's sweet peaks,
my heart in your bosom
finds just what it seeks.

He shouted aloud in his voice pure and strong.
The canyons and mountain tops rang with his song.
The birds and the beasts fled their nests and their lairs.
They scampered away to avoid David's snares.

As David pursued them through hill and through dale,
he chased them around every mountainous trail.
The wolf and the leopard, tiger, lion and bear,
he caught and mixed in with the herd in his care.

And drove them back down to the town of Sassoon,
with rumbling and grunting in mid-afternoon.

The town's folk again were aroused from their chores
by the charging of beasts, they were drawn out of doors:

"Oh, no, get away,"
the young and old cried.
Their hearts in a panic
their work flung aside.

And they fled to their houses, their churches and stores.
They locked up the windows and bolted the doors.
When David arrived and stood in the square,
he looked all about, but no one was there,

"How early you city folk turn in for sleep!
Come, see what's become of the herd in my keep!
For each cow and ox I've brought ten in its stead,
and for each ten you gave me, twenty I've bred.
Hurry up, come on out, and take them away,
or else your new cattle will run and go stray."

But no one came out, the doors didn't budge,
back to the hills, too tired to trudge,
he pulled up a rock and rested his head,
and soon fell asleep, the square for a bed.
When the sun rose, the town's folk emerged.
At old Ohan's house, they quickly converged.

"Ohan, we've had it, now look what he's done.
Our cattle and oxen, he's let loose to run.
He can't tell a lion from an ox or a cow.
Whatever it takes, get rid of him now.
This boy, hear us well, spells nothing but trouble
He'll make our fair town a bear's den and rubble."

IX

Try as he might, he didn't fit in.
The boy was a rebel, Ohan couldn't win.
For David he fixed up a bow and some arrows,
"You're off to the hills to hunt quail and sparrows."
David took up the bow and was ready to roam.
Leaving Sassoon, his folks and his home,
he marched through the barley fields, up the steep trail,
and started to hunt the sparrows and quail.
At dusk he caught sight of a very poor shack,
he sprawled on the floor, the hearth to his back.
In the shack an old woman, who'd known of his dad,
lived alone, without children, and took in the lad.

One day he returned from his regular hunt.
The old woman yelled to him, plainly and blunt,
"I'll be damned, you're his boy, the King's only heir.
You're David, the son of Lion Mher.
I am old and my arms and my legs they are shot.
My worldly possessions are myself and this plot.
So why must you trample it on your sorties
and wreck my year's crops, do tell, if you please?
And what kind of hunter seeks game in these parts?
Seghanasar is the place to practice those arts.
Dzdzmaga was the gate to the King's hunting ground.
There the deer, and the goats, and the wild sheep abound.
Go there, if you're looking to hunt real game,
Instead of round here where the creatures are tame."

"Why do you scold me, in words sharp and base,
I am young, I'd no knowledge of this special place.
Where, please do tell, is the King's hunting ground?"
"Well, go ask your Uncle, he knows where it's found."

X

The next day at dawn he was at Ohan's door.
With his bow in his hand he gave Ohan what for.

"You never said that my dad had a grove,
in the mountains where game used to roam by the drove,
where the rams ran about with the wild goat and deer.
Get up, Uncle Ohan, let's go, is it near?"

"Oh David," cried Ohan, "who told you these things?
May they be struck dumb, oh, how this stings!
That mountain, my lad, is not in our hands.
The game that roamed there have been snatched from
     our lands.
It's not like it was in your dad's blessed day.
And what days those were! Where have they gone?
How many times did we eat venison!
When your father died, God forsook us.
The Melik of Musr then overtook us.
With his troops he attacked, but we were outmanned.
He stole all the game and plundered our land.
Where deer and goats roamed, now there are none.
So it was written, so it was done.
Now it's all past, go back to your work.
If the Melik gets wind of this he'll go beserk."

David scoffed, "The mean Melik can do me no harm.
Why should my inquiries cause him alarm?
Let the Melik of Musr stay in his home.
What business does he have in our parts to roam?
Get up, Uncle Ohan, remember your bow.
To the mountainous hunting ground we've got to go."

So they ventured to Lion Mher's hunting ground,
but when they got there, they heard not a sound.
The trees were cut down, the fences destroyed,
the look-outs laid low, the land was a void.

XI

When it grew dark, they decided to stay.
Ohan of Great Voice had had a long day.
His head on his quiver he rested, then snored.
David however was restless and bored.
His mind was submerged in a deep sea of thought,
when in the dark a shimmering light caught
his eye and he started and jumped to his feet,
and raced toward the light with his legs fast and fleet.
Bounding he ran to the top of the peak,
then he glimpsed a white stone in these parts dark and bleak.
The white marble stone was split in the middle,
and a flame burnt bright there, "What a puzzling riddle!"
Thought David as he ran as fast as he could
to rouse Uncle Ohan to see if he would
wake up and examine this startling sight.

"Uncle Ohan, enough sleep! Come see the light,
settled on top of the mountains afar.
Get up, Uncle Ohan, it's bright as a star
that bobs up and down on a white marble sheet."

Ohan crossed himself twice as he rose to his feet.
"Alas, my poor lad, the light that you've seen,
is all that is left of the altar serene,
of the Church of Our Lady, our keeper and hope.
The convent and church on Maruta's slope,
is called Charkhapan, where your dad went and prayed,
each time he set forth and fierce battle made.

When your father died, God forsook us.
The Melik of Musr then overtook us
Maruta convent he razed to the ground,
but the altar light pierces the darkness profound."

XII

When David discovered the convent's sad fate,
He called to old Ohan, "Dear Uncle, please wait!
I am an orphan, no keeper on earth.
You are my father, though not by birth.

   I want to stay here on Maruta's peak,
until I've rebuilt our convent unique.
Provide me, my keeper, five hundred skilled men,
and five thousand workers to build it again.
Just as it was, we've no time to lose.
Send them this week, please don't refuse."

   Just as he promised, Ohan brought a corps
of five thousand five hundred superior
workers to rebuild the convent on high.
Banging and clanging, it rose to the sky,
just as it was, in all of its glory,
the Church of Our Lady, a blessed promontory.
The monks to the convent quickly returned.
Chanting soared up again, candles were burned.
David came down from the convent sublime
restored to the splendor of Great Mher's time.

XIII

It didn't take long before Melik got word,
"David's the prince now or haven't you heard?
He's rebuilt the convent dear to his dad,
and for seven years now, no tribute you've had."

The Melik exploded and summoned his lords,
"Badin, Gozbadin, claim my just rewards,
Syudin, Charkhadin, set forth straight away.
Leave no stone unturned, Sassoon has to pay
a price for its insolence. Strike hard and swift.
Remind my dear subjects that tribute's no gift.
And bring forty maidens, radiant and bright,
and bring forty short maids of milling height,
and bring forty tall ones my camels to load.
They'll work as my servants and tend my abode."

Gozbadin saluted his master and king,
"Your tribute in gold and the maids we will bring.
Your wish, King of Egypt, is our glad command.
We'll vanquish the rebels in Armenia's land."

The Melik, his wife and his daughter made merry.
They danced and they sang, "Armenia we'll bury.
Gozbadin, the Bold, on Sassoon will make war.
He'll bring us back servants and gold coins galore.
And forty bright maidens and forty short maids,
and forty tall ones, who'll work as our aides.
They'll load up the camels and milk the red cows,

and churn creamy butter and tend the fat sows.
Gozbadin! Gozbadin! our knight, strong and brave,
you'll whip David handily, he's just a knave."
Gozbadin swelled up and nodded with pride,
"Thank you, my ladies, all boasting aside,
if you will with patience my victory await,
we'll have more to dance for, we'll all celebrate."

XIV

With songs and with laughter
his armed men went after,

Sassoon and its people and when they arrived,
Ohan lost his voice and a welcome contrived,

With salt and bread,
with tears and dread,
he bowed down his head
and humbly pled:

"Whatever you want, oh, please, take your pick,
our maids or our hard dug gold in coin or brick,
rosy cheeked maidens, so bright and so fair.
Just don't wreck our lands or rip us asunder.
It's God's realm above and Melik's down under."

Ohan called together the rosy cheeked girls.
Gozbadin checked them out as if they were pearls.

And when he'd selected, he ordered them held
in a locked stable, with pride then he yelled:
"Forty young maidens, radiant and bright,
forty short maidens of milling height,
forty tall maidens the camels to load.
They'll all work as servants in Melik's abode.
With glistening gold our king they'll adorn,
while their friends in Armenia wear black and mourn."

XV

O David! where are you, Armenia's protector?
Dash open the rocks, our convent's erector,
and come to the square, Sassoon's plight is bleak.
And David came down from Maruta's peak
to the old woman's plot where a rusty sword laid,
trampling the turnips, he reached for the blade.

"David, you fool, get out of my garden,"
scowled the old woman, "God beg my pardon,
is my plot the only place that's caught your eye?
A curse on you, David, may you suffer and die.
Just look what you've done, you've levelled my field.
Nothing is left of my winter crop's yield.
What will I live on, can you tell me that?
You're such a foolish and clumsy, spoiled brat.
Were you truly brave, you'd take up your bow,
and rule your dad's realm as he did long ago,
and claim your birthright and live as you ought,

18

for too long you've given Sassoon not a thought.
The Melik's sent forces to sack it today."

"Why do you scold me?" he asked in dismay,
"What does the Melik dare take from me?"

"Everything, David, go home and you'll see.
The Melik is ready to gouge out your eye,
while you're sitting here all alone idly by.
O David, wake up, he's taking it all.
He's sent in his warriors to spread 'round his gall.
Gozbadin and Badin led the attack,
Charkhadin and Syudin brought up the back.
They're plund'ring Sassoon and gathering their loot.
Forty gold sacks is their price for tribute,
and forty young maidens, radiant and bright,
forty short maidens of milling height,
forty tall maidens the camels to load.
They'll all work as servants in Melik's abode."

"Why do you curse me, old woman, pray tell?
Where I can find these fiends, I'll give them hell."

"Where are these fiends? Curse my old ears!
How could this be his son? Brings me to tears!
You're munching on turnips out here in the cold,
while Gozbadin is in your house counting your gold,
and filling the stable with your town's fair maids."
Tossing the turnip, he reached for his blade.
He went to his house, Gozbadin was there,
weighing the gold with cold, greedy care.

Charkhadin and Syudin were holding the bag.
Ohan of Great Voice his tongue didn't wag.
He stood there in silence, his head lowly bowed.
Wringing his hands, he was downcast and cowed.

When David saw this, his eyes flushed with rage.
"Gozbadin, get up, get back in your cage,
This gold is my dad's, it's mine to mete out."

Gozbadin called Ohan, "Rein in this lout.
Are we getting our tribute this minute or what?
If we don't, mark me well, no 'if and or but',
I'll tell the Melik to launch an invasion.
He'll raze Sassoon town, there'll be no dissuasion.
To the ground he will burn it and then plant a park."

But David unfazed did not fear his bark.
"Get out, dogs of Egypt. Flee while you can.
The braves of Sassoon fear no living man.
Did you think we were dead? Or we gave up the ghost?
That you can take tribute and rule us and boast?"

Then David grew angry, and picked up the scales.
He smashed in Gozbadin's head to shrieks and wails.
The shards of the scales pierced holes in the walls,
and fly to this day like sharp, spiked cannon balls.
The warriors of Musr fled, leaving the gold.
Armenia was safe, praise David the bold.
Gozbadin and Badin quickly turned tail.
Charkhadin and Syudin followed their trail.

XVI

"Dear Uncle, how could you, what can I say?
We've great heaps of gold, yet you treat me this way?
You've made me a servant, no keeper on earth,
abandoned to others, is that all I'm worth?"

Ohan lost patience and cried out, "You fool!
The gold was our shield against Melik's fierce rule.
We kept it so that he would turn a kind eye.
You'll see what will happen when we defy.
He'll ruin Sassoon and plunder our land.
Who can oppose him, his onslaught withstand?"

"Hold it, dear Uncle, he'll answer to me,
I'm not afraid of him, just wait and see."
Then he knocked down the door to the dark,
dreary stable, and rescued the maids, before Ohan was able
to say one more word. David told them with glee,
"Long life wish for David, go home, you are free!"

XVII

Battered and bloodied,
tattered and muddied,
the warriors of Egypt fled toward their home soil.
Glimpsing their coming caused noise and turmoil.
The women of Egypt first shouted in joy.
They clapped from their rooftops, "Ahoy, there, ahoy."

They're coming, they're coming, our gold they have brought.
Gozbadin to Sassoon a lesson has taught.
They've brought forty maidens our red cows to tend.
This spring they'll churn butter, our clothing they'll mend.
But as they approached, it soon became clear,
the clapping went silent, something's wrong here.

    The women rushed forward and sassily taunted,
"Gozbadin, you braggard, you're not quite as vaunted,
as boasted and toasted before your excursion.
You ran cross the mountain tops for your diversion?
So tell us, what's up, that your head's split in two?
And where are the maidens and where is your crew?
The forty tall maids and sacks full of gold?
And the rout of Armenia that you foretold?
You went off to Sassoon like a wolf in the wild,
and came back a poor dog, frightened and mild."

    Gozbadin exploded with loud rage and fury,
"Shut up, all you ingrates, I'll be the jury.
You've never seen men like the men of Sassoon.
Each fiercer and stronger than our whole platoon.
Like mountains they tower; they use logs for arrows,
their country's rock solid, a fort on the narrows.
Even the grass blades are sharper than swords.
They slaughtered three hundred of our fiercest lords."

    After he'd spoken, he went to the king,
running impatiently his news to bring.
The king chuckled feverishly from his high throne,

"Well done, Brave Gozbadin, you're back with your own.
I should reward you for what you have done,
With Egypt's great medal that's bright as the sun,
So where is the booty and where are the maids?"
The King asked Gozbadin, "How were the raids?"

     Embarrassed he shrank, his eyes to the ground,
"Long live the King, by my pledge I am bound,
I barely escaped with my life, O great lord,
Armenia has spawned a man like a horde.
He's crazy, fears nothing, not orders nor might.
He smashed in my head with one blow in our fight.
He said, 'I won't give you the gold of my dad,
and the maids of Armenia, they just can't be had.
There's no place for you in the land of Sassoon.
Let Melik himself come for tribute and boon.
Let him come, and we'll fight it out, just me and him,
Let him come and I'll tear him apart limb from limb.'"

     The Melik of Musr flew into a rage,
"Call my whole army, a war we will wage.
ten thousand kids, new born and male,
ten thousand boys, beardless and pale.
ten thousand lads, growing with time,
ten thousand grooms, enjoying their prime,
ten thousand men with black beards and hair,
ten thousand men with heads grey and bare,
ten thousand buglers our coming to sound,
ten thousand drummers our cadence to pound.
Call them and arm them with sword, bow, and shield.

We'll tame master David and get him to yield.
I'll pillage and plunder Sassoon till it's rubble.
I'll teach Sassoon's people to cause Egypt trouble."

XVIII

The Melik assembled his numberless forces,
and went to Sassoon with arms, men and horses,
and when he arrived, he set up his tent,
some distance from Sassoon, where the horde went
to the river named Batma to quench their great thirst.
So many were they that when they immersed
their mouths in the water, the river went dry,
and the river flow to Sassoon slowed by and by,
until the town's water flow came to a halt.
Distressed, Ohan wondered what was at fault.
Donning his cloak, he searched for the cause.
On a high look out, he took a quick pause,
he saw tents by the thousands, like a blanket of snow,
just as if winter had fallen below.

His warm blood ran cold and his tongue became tied.
Running back home, "God help us," he cried.
"Woe, run away, it has come, it is here!"
"What, my dear Uncle, has caused you such fear?"

"The pain and the fire, you've brought on our heads.
The Melik has come here to tear us to shreds.
His army outnumbers the stars in the sky.

Woe to our lives, woe to our lands!
Gather the maids and gold in our hands.
Let us bow down, perhaps he'll forbear.
Perhaps he'll take pity, his sword he might spare."

"Hold it there, Uncle, don't blink an eye.
You're tired and anxious, now go home and lie
down in your bed, while I take a look
at what Melik's up to." So David took
his leave and ran off to the old woman's shack.

"Hey granny," he shouted, "Look, I've come back.
Quick get your skewers and old iron scraps
to tie on the donkey with these tattered straps.
I'm taking on Melik the way you once said.

"O, David," she cried, "God strike me dead.
How could your father have had such a lad?
When he went to war, a great horse he had,
a fiery steed and a waistband of gold.
And in his right hand a cross he would hold.
He had a mail shirt, defense to afford.
and a thick metal helmet and bright Lightning Sword.
And you're off to battle with donkey and skewer."

"Okay, okay, granny, your words could be fewer,
if you would just tell me the place where it's hid."

"Go, ask your uncle, you're not just a kid.
Tell him to get it, and bring it to you.
And if he refuses, you'll just have to do
whatever it takes to gather his trust,
but get what is yours, as is mete and is just."

XIX

David went home to his Uncle directly,
"Hey Uncle," he shouted loud and suspectly,
"My father had armor of which I was told,
and a fiery steed and a waistband of gold
and in his right hand a cross he would bear,
so as he made battle, he gave life no care.
He had a mail shirt, defense to afford,
and a thick metal helmet and bright Lightning Sword.
Wherever they are, Uncle, give them to me."

"O David, my David, say how can this be?"
Ohan cried in dread, "But since your dad died,
no one has taken the horse for a ride,
nor has the sword been out of its case,
nor the mail shirt, nor the gold mace.
Just leave me alone, don't torment me.
Take them, and use them, they're your legacy."

XX

David put on the armor and buckled the band.
He donned the mail shirt, his sword in his hand.
And raising the victory cross to the sky,
he mounted the Lion's steed and riding high,
with a snap of his whip, he galloped away,
and Ohan of Great Voice, wept for this day,

"Ten thousand woes, for the steed he has taken.
Ten thousand woes, for the gold he's forsaken.
Ten thousand woes, for the mail shirt he's wearing.
Ten thousand woes, for the sword he is bearing."

On hearing this, David boiled up with rage.
He turned the steed back and charged to engage
his Uncle's attention, making him smart.
Poor Ohan in fear changed his tune and his heart:

"Alas, my David, poor David, is lost.
Alas, he is lost at such a high cost."

When David heard this, he sighed and calmed down.
He jumped from the horse and touched Ohan's gown.
He then kissed his hand, and Ohan of Great Voice
with fatherly care and a nod did rejoice
at the sight of this youth, and bid him farewell,
and sent him away Musr Melik to quell.

XXI

David's mom had a brother whose name was Toros.
This uncle's fierce exploits unfolded before us.
When Toros got wind of the up-coming battle,
he pulled up a tree and slaughtered some cattle,
and then in the distance he was heard yelling:

"You on the plain with your tents I am telling,
David of Sassoon's coming your way.
How many are you? You don't want to stay.

What are you waiting for? Haven't you heard?
He flies on his steed like a great preying bird.
Get away, while you've time, before he arrives.
I'm warning you, go, if you value your lives."

Then from his shoulder he took the tree trunk,
and swinging it, cleared them away with one dunk.
From the peak David watched and then fiercely roared
like a dragon to wake up Melik and his horde:

"If you're asleep, you'd better wake up,
and if you're awake, you'd better stand up,
and if you are standing, you'd better gear up,
and if you are geared up, you'd better mount up,
and if you are mounted, you'd better ride on,
and don't complain later that we were spied on,
while David attacked like a thief in the night.
So wake up, get ready, you're in for a fight."

Making his challenge, he spurred on his steed.
And with shocking bolts down from a cloud,
the Lightning Sword glistening followed his lead,
and struck in the midst of the Melik's fierce crowd.

David wreaked mayhem the first half the day,
and the rush of their blood like a rising red tide,
Melik's men by the thousands carried away,
both dead and alive in human landslide.

In the midst of the carnage was an old man,
who'd seen much of life and was known as a sage.
"Boys," said he, "Step aside, quick, so I can
go and see David and quiet his rage."

The old man set off to plead for his band.
He went before David, "O brave one," he said,
"May your fist remain strong, with a sword in your hand.
May your sword remain sharp, like the thoughts in your
    head.
Pray hear me out though I'm old and I'm weak,
and weigh my words well as our lives you determine.
What have we done that you willfully wreak
death and destruction and kill us like vermin?

Each one among us is some mother's son.
Each one among us is some household's light,
who's left his dear wife and his housework undone,
her wet eyes are fixed on the road in deep fright.

His children lie shivering in their cold beds.
His parents are poor, bent over and old.
With crying and mourning, veils over their heads,
the young brides are waiting their grooms to behold.

Melik gathered these men upon pain of death.
He ordered them here crushing their will.
They're miserable conscripts who've breathed their last
    breath.
What harm can they do you? They bear you no ill.

So pity us peons, mean Melik's your foe.
If you've got a bone to pick, then in God's name,
you two should cross swords and fight toe to toe,
and spare us unfortunate pawns in your game."

"Well spoken, old man, you are wise as your age,"
David said to the grey beard at Sassoon's high gate,
"But where's the mean Melik that I might engage
in one-on-one combat and seal his dark fate."

"You see the great tent? That's where he sleeps,
the one with the smoke coming out of the top.
It's not real smoke, but a foul fume that seeps,
out of his mouth as he sleeps without stop."

Not a moment to spare, David mounted his steed.
He rode to the tent where the mean Melik lay.
At the door of the tent he arrived with great speed,
and roared at the guards who cringed in dismay.

"Where is he hiding who threatens my lands?
Call him out, in the open, we'll fight on this field.
If he isn't dead now, he'll die at my hands.
His match he has met, his fate is now sealed."

"The Melik," they said, "Is in a deep slumber.
For seven full days his post he's forsaken.
So far just three days have passed of that number.
Four more still remain before he'll awaken."

"You mean to tell me he naps while his men
are swimming in blood as deep as the sea?
For seven full days he snores in his den,
while he sends his poor troops to do battle with me.

Sleep-shmeep hear me well, this is insane.
Get him up, send him out, we shall meet in the square.
I'll give him sleep in which he'll remain
forever at rest with a tomb for a lair."

The guards were now shaken and picked up a spear.
They heated it red in the campfire's heat.
Their king snored so loud that he couldn't hear,
as they put the hot spear to the soles of his feet.

"How can a man get a decent night's rest
as long as these damned fleas are swarming around."
The giant king muttered, then undistressed,
he turned himself over and slept on the ground.

So they got a huge plow from a field near the tent,
and they heated its blade on the blazing red fire,
and when it glowed bright and iridescent,
they put it against the back of their sire.

"How can a man get a decent night's rest,
as long as these blasted mosquitoes do flit?"
Groggy, he rubbed his eyes, glimpsing a guest.
It was David who'd come to pay a visit.

He raised his head up and muttered a curse,
then he blew upon David to sweep him away,
He huffed and he puffed, but he could not coerce,
David to leave, so he shrank in dismay.

Amazement and fear engulfed his cold heart,
seeing how David withstood his fierce blows.
His bloody red eyes were fixed like a dart,
as he frowned upon David and cast a mean pose.

Seeing that David did not flinch at all,
his beastly strength drained like a wilting bean stalk.
So he sat up and thought of a way he could stall,
and he put on a smile and started to talk.

"Greetings, dear David, come in, take a chair,
you must be quite tired, let's have a good chat.
If you're still intent upon settling this affair,
we'll fight one on one, okay, how is that?"

Under his tent the wily old troll
had dug a great pit some forty feet deep.
He'd had a net flung across the wide hole
with a rug for a cover, his secret to keep.

Whomever he couldn't defeat in combat
he lured to his tent to catch in his snare.
Asking them in as his guests just like that,
they would fall in the pit as they sat unaware.

So David dismounted from his tall horse
and went and sat down upon the guest's rug.
It gave way and he fell as a matter of course
into the pit that Melik had dug.

Melik cackled and smirked at the fate of his guest.
He ordered a millstone to close off the pit.
"You can rot in the dark, my noisome young pest,
for the rest of your life in my snare you shall sit."

XXII

Ohan of Great Voice slept poorly that night.
Dark dreams filled his head like an unruly crowd.
O'er Egypt the sun rose with radiant light,
but a black cloud hung over Sassoon like a shroud.

Stricken with terror he jumped from his bed.
"Oh, Wife, light a candle, take hold of my hand.

It's David, I know it, dark fate on our head.
A black cloud's descending upon our dear land."

"I'll kill him, I tell you," scowled his wife.
"Who knows where he is, the reckless ingrate?
While you're here at home afraid for your life,
tormented by dreams about others' fate."

Ohan fell asleep, but was wakened again.
"O, Wife, hear me out, David's in a tight spot.
The star over Egypt shines brighter than ten,
while Sassoon's star fades away like a dot."

"Dammit, old man, it's after midnight,"
His wife scolded loudly, sharply and tart.
Ohan crossed himself, not wanting a fight,
and fell back to sleep, though troubled at heart.

He then dreamt a dream that was yet darker still.
He saw in the heavenly skyscape on high
that Egypt's bright star was yet more visible,
while Sassoon's was falling down out of the sky.

This time he awoke in tortured chagrin,
"A curse on your house, why'd I listen to you?
David's in danger, he's my last of kin.
Now get me my armor I've got work to do."

XXIII

Ohan rose from bed and went to the stable.
He gave the white horse a kind slap on the back.
"Tell me old whitey, how fast are you able,
to get me to David to join the attack?"

"You'll get there by morning if you ride on me."
said the horse to Ohan, belly slumped to the ground.
"And what good is that? Shall I go there to be
in time for the mass at his burial mound?"

He then gave the red horse a slap on the saddle.
He too dropped its belly down to the ground.
"Dear red horse, how soon can we join in the battle
and fight on the field where David is found?"

The red horse responded, "In less than an hour,
you'll be there with David engaged in the battle,"
"A curse on your fodder and may it grow sour,
for nought have I fed you, I've no time to prattle."

Next Ohan turned to inspect the black steed.
He too dropped his belly down to the ground,
so, my black beauty, in my time of need,
can you take me there, where David is bound?

"If you wrap your legs tight and get a good grip,"
said the black horse, jumping out of his stall,
"Before your foot's through the second stirrup,
you'll be there with David, hold on or you'll fall."

XXIV

He led the black horse out for the trip,
mounting him quickly from the left side.
Before his right foot was through the stirrup,
atop Sassoon's peaks they'd gone for a ride.

And there Ohan saw David's horse was forsaken,
neighing and wandering through the high leas.
Below Melik's camp was teeming with men,
endlessly streaming like waves on the seas.

He girded his waist with seven ox skins
to hold in the pressure that filled in his cheek.
He puffed like a cloud when the thunder begins
and roared from atop Sassoon's highest peak.

"Hey, David, Ho, David, wherever you are,
remember the cross of the great sacrifice,
and call out the name of Our Lady afar,
you'll see light of day if you heed this advice."

His voice rumbled loudly from heaven to earth
and reached David's ear in the pit dark and bleak.
"Hey, hey," David said, with great joy and mirth,
"That's my uncle's loud voice calling from Sassoon's peak."

"In the name of Our Lady on Maruta's height,
and the immortal cross of the great sacrifice,
I call on you now to ease David's plight."
So bellowed he forth, in a voice that could slice.

And slice it did, for when it hit,
the millstone was shattered in thousands of parts,
uncovering the mouth of the deep and dark pit,
sending fragments to orbit like stone-hewn darts.

David rose from the pit and stood bold and wild.
Melik shuddered in fear and started to squawk,
"David, my brother, let's be reconciled,
Let's sup together and have a good talk."

"No more shall I sit at the table with you,
you subhuman, cowardly, wily old man.
Now go get your arms with no more ado,
and come to the square as fast as you can."

"Have it your way," said the Melik with spite,
"But on one condition, the first blow is mine."
Setting out for the square, David shouted,
"All right, take your best shot, 'cause the next one is mine."

So they stood face to face in the midst of the square.
Melik mounted his horse with his lance in his hand.
To Diyarbekir town he rode to prepare,
for his charge against David, to make his last stand.

With clashing and tremors the great charge began.
With the force of three thousand huge stones his lance hit.
The earth shook and wobbled as Egypt's king ran
and the impact raised clouds of thick dust and grey grit.

"An earthquake has struck," said the people aghast,
frightened in far off lands jarred by the blows.
"No," said some others, "It's just some great blast,
caused by the clash between two mortal foes."

"I've struck David dead, with only one blow,"
Melik bragged to his men, smug with conceit.
"Don't be so sure, I'm next to go,"
said David unfazed, "I'm still on my feet."

Melik stammered, "I started too close the first time.
Next time I'll get you, I'll build up some speed."
Melik mounted his horse and started to climb
over the hills to a far land indeed.

This time from Aleppo he spurred on his horse,
and stirred up a storm, lightning, thunder and rain,
and shaking the world with yet greater force,
he started his charge with grunting and strain.

He came and he struck, and the sound of the blow
left the people close by as deaf as a stone.
"The House of Sassoon is finally laid low,"
the Melik declared with a snide, haughty tone.

"Not so fast," called out David, "I'm still on my feet.
Now you've had your turn, this time I will go."
"Just one more time and you'll meet your defeat,
I started too close and was charging too slow."

The third time Melik went back to his home,
and starting from Egypt he charged with his lance.
Spurring his horse across the sea foam,
he took aim at David across the expanse.

He struck him once more with all of his strength,
a huge, heavy blow packing hundreds of tons.
The impact unsettled Sassoon's breadth and length,
raising a dust cloud that darkened the sun.

Three days and three nights dust darkened the skies,
hanging about like an ominous sign.
Three days and three nights, there were wailing and sighs,
mourning the death of their nation's scion.

Then on the third day, in the midst of the dust,
David emerged, like a peak through a cloud.
Majestic and tall, standing like a stone bust,
he shouted to Melik, who was shaken and cowed.

"Melik," he said, "Guess whose turn it is next;
hope you are ready to meet your demise."
Melik's heart trembled as though he were hexed,
and the haughty king's ego was cut down to size.

Melik fled to a pit in the earth's darker zones,
which he'd dug for himself in terror and fear.
He sealed it securely with forty millstones,
and forty thick skins of oxen and deer.

A lion was David, like his father Mher,
growling, he rose to set things aright.
He mounted his horse, storming into the air,
with the great Lightning Sword in his hand glistening bright.

Melik's wicked old mother came to entreat
David for mercy, distraught, with wild hair,
"My hair, sire David, trample under your feet,
I'll bear your first blow, if my son you will spare."

David was poised to strike the next blow.
Melik's sister came forth to settle the strife.
"Your sword's second cut, I'll undergo,
straight through my heart, just spare him his life."

The time had arrived to strike the third blow,
"Let no one dare come and stand in my way.
With God's help we'll at last be rid of this foe,
but I must strike now with no further delay."

And strike he did, with fury and sound,
on his fiery steed he soared through the sky,
A lightning bolt flew from his sword to the ground,
with such force it was certain that Melik would die.

The lightning bolt struck on the seals to the pit,
piercing the skins and the stones through and through.
It struck Melik's heart and soon as it hit,
it severed the fiendish king's body in two.

Melik then called from his dark hiding place,
"I'm still alive. Hit me once more."
When David heard this, he screwed up his face,
knowing the force that the Lightning Sword bore.

"Melik," he said, "Get up, move a bit."
As Melik arose and cautiously crept,
a hole opened up in the place he'd been hit,
and his body collapsed in two as he stepped.

When Melik's troops saw what had become,
of their miserable leader, they scrambled in fear.
David promised them pardon if they'd succumb
and urged them sincerely to lend him an ear.

"Heed me, men of Egypt, you're tillers of soil.
You're hungry and tired, you're longing for home.
Why have you come to Sassoon to despoil
our land and our people? Why do you roam?

You've a thousand and one worries and pains.
You've a thousand and one troubles to bear.
We too have our homes, our families and strains.
We too have our young and our old who need care.

Can you explain why you've traipsed over here?
Are you restless and bored with your calm peaceful lives?
Your land and your kinfolk, aren't they dear?
Have you tired of tilling your fields so they thrive?

By the route that you came here, you now must go back
to your homeland of Musr in Egypt afar.
But be warned if you ever raise arms and attack
us again by some ruinous, ill-fated star,

No pit that you dig can be dug deep enough.
no millstones you stack can be piled high enough,
to spare you the wrath of this son of Sassoon
or the bright Lightning Sword with its piercing typhoon.

Then only God will know,
who will regret it more,
we, who must go to war,
or you, who made us your foe."

Յովհաննէս Թումանեանի

Սասունցի Դաւիթը

I

Առիծ-Մրհերը՝ զարմով դիւցազուն՝
Քառասուն տարի իշխում էր Սասուն.
Իշխում էր ահեղ, ու նրրա օրով
Հաւքն էլ չէր անցնում Սասմայ սարերով:
Սասմայ սարերից չա՛տ ու շատ հեռու
Թրնդում էր նրրա հրռչակն ահարկու,
Խսաում էր իր փառքն, արարքն անվեհեր.
Հազար բերան էր—մի Առիծ Մրհեր:

II

Էսպէս, ահաւոր առիծի նրման,
Սասմայ սարերում նրաաած էր իշխան
Քառասուն տարի: Քառասուն տարում
«Ա՛խ» չէր քաշել նա դեռ իրեն օրում.
Բայց հիմի, երբ որ եկաւ ծերացաւ,
Էն անահ սիրտր ներս սողաց մի ցաւ:
— Հասել են կեանքիս աշնան օրերր,
Շուտով սեւ հողին կ՚երթամ ես գերի,
Կ՚անցնի ծխի պէս փառքր Մրհերի,
Կ՚անցնեն է՛լ անունն, է՛լ սարասափի, է՛լ ահ,
Իմ անտէր ու որբ աշխարքի վրրա
Ոտի կր կանգնեն հազար քաջ ու դեւ...
Մի ժառանգ չունեմ՝ իմ անցման եաեւ
Իմ թուրր կապի, Սասուն պահպանի...
Ու միտք էր անում հրական ծերունի:

Մի օր էլ՝ էն գործ յօնքերը կիտած
Երբ միտք էր անում, երկնքից յանկարծ
Մի հուր-հրրեղէն յայտնուեց քաջին,
Ոտները ամպոտ կանգնեց առաջին:
— Ողջո՞յն մեծագոր Սասմայ հրսկային,
Քու ձէնը հասաւ Աստրծու գահին,
Ու շուտով Նա քեզ մի զաւակ կը տայ:
Բայց լաւ իմանաս, լեռների՛ արքայ,
Որ օրը որ քեզ ժառանգ է տրուել,
Էն օր կը մեռնէք քու կինն էլ, դու էլ:

— Իր կամքը լինի, ասաւ Մհերը.
Մենք մահինն ենք միշտ ու մահր մերը,
Բայց որ աշխարքում ժառանգ ունենանք,
Մենք էլ նրրանով անմեռ կը մրնանք:
Հրրեշտակն էստեղ ցոլացաւ նորից,
Ու էս երջանիկ աւետման օրից
Երբ իննը ամիս, իննը ժամն անցաւ,
Առիծ-Մհերը զաւակ ունեցաւ:
Դալիթ անուանեց իրեն կորիւնին,
Կանչեց իր եղբայր Ջէնով Օհանին,
Երկիրն ու որդին աւանդեց նրրան,
Ու կինն էլ, ինքն էլ էն օրը մեռան:

IV

Էս դարում Մրսրը՝ անյաղթ ու հզոր
Մրսրա-Մելիքն էր նրստած թագաւոր,
Երբոր իմացաւ՝ էլ Մրհեր չրկայ,
Վերկացաւ կրւով Սասունի վրրա:
Չէնով-Օհանը ահից սարսափած՝
Թշնամու առաջն ելաւ գրլխաբաց,
Ադաչանք արաւ, ընկաւ ոտներր.
— Դո՛ւ ելիր, ասաւ, մեր գրլխի տերր,
Ու քու շրւաքում քանի որ մենք կանք,
Քու ծառան լինենք, քու խարջր մշտ տանք,
Միայն մեր երկիր քարուքանդ չանես
Ու բաղցրր աչքով մեզ մրտիկ անես:
— Չէ՛, ասաւ Մելիք, քու ամբողջ ազգով
Անց պիտի կենաս իմ թրրի տակով,
Որ էզուց-էլոր ինչ էլ որ անեմ,
Ոչ մի սասունցի թուր չառնի իմ դեմ:
Ու գրնաց Օհան, բոլոր-բովանդակ
Սասունը բերաւ, քաշեց թրրի տակ.
Մենակ Դաւիթր, ինչ արին-չարին,
Մօտ չեկաւ Մրսրա-Մելիքի թրրին:
Եկան, քաշեցին՝ թէ զօրով տանեն,
Թափի տրւաւ, մարդկանց գրցեց դես ու դեն,
Փոքրիկ ճրկույթր մի քարի առաւ,
Ապառաժ քարից կրրակ դուրս թրռաւ:
— Պէտք է րսպանեմ էս փոքրիկ ծուռին,
Ասաւ թագաւորն իրեն մեծերին:
— Թագաւ՛ր, ասին, դու էշքան հրզոր,
Թրրիդ տակին է ողջ Սասուն էսոր.

Ի՞նչ պետք է անի քեզ մի երեխայ,
Թէկուզ իր տեղով հիանգ կըրակ դառնայ:
— Դն'ւք գիտէք, ասաւ Մրսրայ թագաւոր,
Բայց թէ իմ գըլխին փորձանք գայ մի օր,
Էս օրը վրկայ,
Սըրրանից կը գայ:

V

Էս որ պատահեց, մեր Դաւիթ հրսկան
Մի մանուկ էր դեռ եօթ-ութ տարեկան.
Մանուկ եմ ասում, բայց էնքան ուժեղ,
Որ նըրա համար թէ մարդ,—թէ' մրժեղ:
Բայց վա՜յ խեղձ որբին աշխարքի վրրա,
Թէկուզ Առիւծի կորիւն լինի նա:
Չէնով Օհանին ունէր մի չար կին:
Մին-երկու լըռեց, մի օր էլ կարգին
Իրեն մարդու հետ սկրսաւ կըռուել.
— Էս մենակ հոգի, հազար ցաւի տէր:
Ի՞նչ ես ուրիշի եթիմը բերել,
Նըրստեցրել գըլխիս պարապ հացակեր...
Հո՞դեմ գըլուխը... էս գերի հո չէ՞մ՝
Ամէնքի քէֆի եւետիգ թըրշեմ...
Մի կուտ կորցըրրո՛ւ, կարգի՛ր մի բանի,
Գընա, իր համար աշխատանք անի...
Ու հետն սկրսաւ ողբալ ու կոծել,
Իր օրը սրգալ, իր բախտն անիծել,
Թէ անբախտ եղաւ աշխարքի միջում,
Ոչ մի տէր ունի, ոչ մարդն է խրղճում...

48

Գրնաց Օհանը երեիսի ոտի
Մի զույգ ոտնաման բերավ երկաթի,
Երկաթի մի կող շալակին դրրած,
Ու արավ Սասմայ քաղքի զառնարած։

VI

Քըշեց զառները մեր հովիւ հրական,
Ելաւ Սասունի սարերն աննրման։
        «Է՜յ ջան, սարե՜ր,
        Սասման սարե՜ր ...»
Որ կանչեց, նրրա ձէնից ահաւոր
Դղորդ-դըմբըրըմբոցն ընկաւ սար ու ձոր,
Վայրի գազաններ բրներից փախան,
Քարէքար ընկան, դատարկուն եղան։
Դավիթն էլ ընկաւ նրրանց ետեւից,
Որին մի սարից, որին մի ձորից—
Աղուես, նապաստակ, գէլ, եղնիկ բրռնեց,
Հաւաքեց, բերաւ, զառներին խառնեց,
Իրիկւան քըշեց ողջ Սասմայ քաղաք։
Կաղկա՜նձ ու ռռնձ՜գ, աղմո՜ւկ, աղաղա՜կ ...
Քաղքըցիք յանկարծ մին էլ էն տեսան՝
Գալիս են հրրեւս աննհամար գազան։
        «Վա՜յ, հարա՜յ, փախէ՜ք ...
        Մեծեր, երեիսէք
        Սրտաճաք եղաձ,
        Գործները թողաձ,»
Որը տուն ընկաւ, որը ժամ, խանութ,
Ու ամուր փակեց դուռն ու լուսամուտ։

49

Դավիթը եկավ, կանգնեց մեյդանում.
— Վա՜հ, էս մարդիկը ի՞նչ վատ են քըրնում.
       Հէ՜յ ուլատեր, հէ՜յ զառնատեր.
       Ելէ՜ք, շուտով բացէք դռներ.
       Ով մինն ունէր—տասն եմ բերել,
       Ով տասն ունէր—քըրսանն արել ...
       Շուտով ելէ՜ք, եկէ՜ք, տարէ՜ք,
       Ձեր զառն ու ուլ գոմերն արէք:
Տեսաւ՝ չեն գալի, դուռ չեն բաց անում.
Ինքն էլ մեկնըւեց քաղքի մեյդանում,
Գըլուխը դըրաւ մի քարի՝ մըռաց
Ու մուշ-մուշ քընեց մինչեւ լուսաբաց:
Լուսին իշխաններ եկան միասին,
Գընացին Ձէնով Օհանին ասին.
— Sո՜ Ձէնով Օհան, տո՛ մահի տարած,
Էս խենթը բերիր, արիր զառնարած,
Ոչ զառն է ջոկում, ոչ գէն ու աղէս,
Գազանով լցրեց մեր քաղաքն էսպէս.
Աստուած կը սիրես՝ դի՛ր ուրիշ բանի,
Թէ չէ էս խա՜լխին լեղաճաք կանի:

VII

       Ելաւ Դաւթի մօտ գընաց Օհանը.
— Հօրեղբայր Օհան, հեռո՛ւ եկ, կամա՛ց,
Ուլեր կը փախչէն:—Մին էլ էնտեղից
Մի բոզ նապաստակ, ականջները ցից,
Խըրտնեց ու անհից դուրս պրծաւ յանկարծ.
Դաւիթն էր. ելաւ, էտեւից ընկած

Էն սարը քրշեց, ետ բերաւ էս ձոր,
Բերաւ, ուլերին խառնեց նորից նոր:
— Օ՜ֆ, ի՜նչ դրժար է, հորեղբայր Օհան.
Աստուած օխնել է էս սեւ-սեւ ուլեր,
Ամա բոզալուկ էս ուլեր, որ կան,
Փախչում են, ցրրում ողջ սարերն ի վեր.
Էնքան եմ երեկ վազել, չարչարուե՜լ,
Մ'ինչեւ հաւաքել ու տուն եմ բերե՜լ...
    Նայեց Օհանը, որ Դաւթի հագին
Ռտնամման չի էլ մրնացել կարգին,
Մահակն էլ մաշել, մինչ բունն է հասել,
Մի օրւայ միջում էնքան է վազել:
— Դալի՛թ ջան, ասաւ, չեմ թողնի էսպես,
Բոզալուկ ուլեր չարչարում են քեզ.
Էգուց նախիրը կը տանես արոտ:
    Ասաւ Օհանը ու միս առաւոտ
Գրնաց, նորից նոր մեր Դաւթի ոտի
Մի ջուխտ նոր տրրեխս բերաւ երկաթի,
Երկաթի մի կոռ հարիր լրդրական
Ու շինեց Սասմայ քաղքի նախրապան:

VIII

    Քրշեց նախիրը մեր նախրորդ հրսկան,
Ելաւ Սասունի սարերն աննրման:
        «Է՜յ ջան, սարեր,
        Սասման սարե՜ր,
        Ի՜նչ անուշ է
        Ձեր լանջն ի վեր»...

Որ կանչեց, նըրա ձէնից ահատոր
Դըղորդ-դըմբըրըմբըցն ընկաւ սար ու ձոր։
Վայրի գազաններ բըներից փախան,
Քարէքար ընկան, դատարկուն եղան։
Դալիֆն էր. ընկաւ նրանց եռեւից,
Որին մի սարից, որին մի ձորից,
Գէլ, ինձ, առիւծ, արջ. վագըր բըրնեց,
Հաւաքեց, բերաւ, իր նախրին խառնեց
Ու առաջն արաւ դէպ Սասմայ քաղաք։
Ոռնո՛ց, մըոռընչի՛ւն, աղմո՛ւկ, աղաղա՛կ ...
Վախկոտ քաղքըցիք մին էլ ի՞նչ տեսան,
Հէնց քաղքի վըրայ անհամար գազան ...
        «Վա՛յ, հարա՛յ, փախէ՛ք ...»
        Մեծեր, երեխէք
        Սրրտաճաք եղած,
        Գործները թողած
Փախան, ներս ընկան տուն, ժամ կամ խանութ,
Ամուր փակեցին դուռ կամ լուսամուտ։
Դալիթը եկաւ կանգնեց մէյդանում.
— Վա՛հ, էս քաղքըցիք ի՞նչ վաղ են քը).նում։
        Հէ՛յ կովատէր, հի՛է՛յ գոմշատէր,
        Ելէ՛ք, շուտով բացէք դըռներ,
        Ով մինն ունէր — տասն եմ բերել,
        Ով տասն ունէր — քրասնն արել։
        Շուտով ելէ՛ք, եկէ՛ք, տարէ՛ք,
        Ձեր եզն ու կով գոմերն արէք։
Տեսաւ՝ չեն գալի, դուռ չեն բաց անում,
Ինքն էլ մեկնւեց քաղքի մէյդանում,
Գըլուխը դըրաւ մի քարի, մընաց,
Ու մուշ-մուշ քրնեց մինչեւ լուսաբաց։

Լուսին իշխաններ եկան միասին,
Գրնացին Ջէնով Օհանին ասին.
— Ամա՛ն, քեզ մատաղ, ա՛յ Օհան ախպէր,
Մեր եզն ու մեր կով թող մրնան անտէր,
Միայն սրանից ազատ արա մեզ:
Ոչ արջն է ջոկում, ոչ գոմէշն ու եզ,
Մի օր էս քաղքին փորձանք կը բերի,
Արջերոց կանի, կը տայ կաւերի:

IX

Դաւիթ չրդառաւ, մի կրրա՛կ դառաւ:
Ճարը կրտրրուած՝ Օհանը բերաւ
Նետ-աղեղ շինեց ու տրւաւ իրեն՝
Գրնալ, որս անի սարերի վրրէն:
Դաւիթ նետ-աղեղն առաւ Օհանից,
Հեռացաւ Սասմայ քաղքի սահմանից
Ու դառաւ որսկան: Գնաց, մի կորկում
Լոր էր սպանում, ճնճղուկ էր զարկում,
Մրթանը գրնում իրեն հոր ծանոթ
Աղքատ, անողի մի ծեր կրնկայ մօտ,
Վիշապի նրման, երկա՛ր, ահա՛ գին
Մեկնրւում, քրնում կրրակի կողքին:
Մի օր էլ, երբ որ իր որսից դառձաւ,
Պառաւր վրրէն սառտիկ բարկացաւ.
— Վա՛յ Դաւիթ, ասաւ, մահրս տանի քեզ,
Դո՞ւ պէտք է էն հոր զաւակը լինե՛ս:
Չեռից ու ոտից րնկած մի ծեր կին—
Ես եմ ու էն արտն Աստրծու տակին.

Ինչո՞ւ ես գրնում, տափում, տրրորում,
Իմ ամբողջ տարւան ապրուստը կրտրում:
Թէ որսկան ես դու — նետ-աղեղրդ ա՛ռ,
Ծրծմակայ գլխից մինչեւ Սեղանսար
Քու հէրը ձեռքին մի աշխարհ ունէր,
Որսով մէջը լի որսի սար ունէր.
Եղնիկ կայ էնտեղ, այծեամ ու պախրայ.
Կարո՞դ ես — գրնա, էնտեղ որս արա:
— Ի՞նչ ես, ա՛յ պառաւ, էլ ինձ անիծում.
Ես ջահիլ եմ դեռ, ես նոր եմ լրսում:
Ո՞րտեղ է հապա սարը մեր որսի ...
— Գրնա՛, հօրեղբայրդ—Օհանը կասի:

X

Հօրեղբօր շէմքում միա օրը ծէգին
Դալիթը կանգնեց աղեղը ձեռքին:
— Հօրեղբա՛յր Օհան, ինչո՞ւ չես ասել՝
Իմ հէրը որսի սար է ունեցել,
Այծեամ կայ էնտեղ, եղջերու, կրխտար.
Վեր կաց, հօրեղբա՛յր, տար ինձ որսասար:
— Վա՛յ, կանչեց Օհան, էդ քու խոսքը չէր,
Էդ ով քեզ ասաւ, լեզուն պապանձւէր:
Էն սարը, որդի՛, գրնաց մեր ձեռից,
Էն սարի որսն էլ գրնաց էն սարից,
Էլ չկան այծեամ, եղջերու, կրխտար:
Քանի լուսեղէն քու հէրը դեռ կար,
(Է՛յ գիտի օրեր — ո՞րտեղ էք կորել,)
Ես շատ եմ էնտեղ որսի միս կերել ...

54

Քու հէրը մեռաւ, Աստուած խռովեց,
Սրսրայ թագաւոր զօրքեր ժողովեց,
Եկաւ, մեր երկիր քարուքանդ արաւ,
Էս սարի որսն էլ թալանեց, տարաւ։
Եղնիկը գռնաց, եղջերուն գռնաց ...
Մեր գիրն էլ հալբաթ էսպէս էր գրած։
Անցել է, որդի, քու բանին գռնա,
Սրսրայ թագաւոր ձէնրդ կ'իմանայ ...
— Սրսրայ թագաւոր ինձ ի՞նչ կ'անի որ ...
Ես ի՞նչ եմ հարցնում Սրսրայ թագաւոր։
Սրսրայ թագաւոր թող Սրսրը կենայ,
Իմ հօր սարերում ի՞նչ գործ ունի նա ...
Վեր կաց, հօրեղբա'յր, նետ-աղեղդ առ,
Կապարճրդ կապի'ր, գռնանք որսասար։
     Ելաւ Օհանը ճարը կտրրւած,
Գռնացին տեսան՝ էլ ի՞նչ որսասար։
Անտառը ջարդած, պարիսպն աւերած,
Բուրգերը արած գետնին հաւասար ...

XI

Գիշերը հասաւ, մրնացին էնտեղ։
Զէնով Օհանն էր, իր նետն ու աղեղ
Դրրաւ գլխի տակ, հանգիստ խրորմփաց։
Դաւիթր մրնաց մրտքի ծովն ընկած։
Մին էլ նկատեց, որ մութր հեռուում
Մի թէժ, փայլփլուն կրրակ է վառում։
Էն լուսր բրրնած՝
Վեր կացաւ, գռնաց,

Գրնաց ու գրնա՛ց, բարձրացաւ մի սար,
Բարձրացաւ, տեսաւ մի մեծ մարմար քար
Կիսից պատռռուած,
Ու միջից վառուած
Բրխում է լուսը պա՛րգ, քուլա-քուլա՛,
Բարձրանում, իջնում ետ քարի վրրա։
Վար իջաւ Դաւիթ էնտեղից կրրկին,
Վար իջաւ, կանչեց Չէնով Օհանին:
— Ե՛լ, հորեղբա՛յր, քանի՛ քրնես,
Ե՛լ, էն պայծառ լուսը մի տես։
Լուս է իջել բարձըր սարին,
Բարձըր սարին, մարմար քարին:
Ե՛լ, հորեղբայր, անուշ քրնից.
էն ի՞նչ լուս է բրխում քարից:
        Ելաւ, խաչ քաշեց Օհանն երեսին։
Ե՛յ, որդի՛, ասաւ, մեռնեմ իր լուսին,
էն մեր Մարութայ սարն է զօրաւոր:
էն լուսի տեղը կանգնած էր մի օր
Սասմայ ապաւէն, Սասմայ պահապան
Մեր Սուրբ Տիրամօր վանքը Չարխափան:
Մըշտական, երբ որ կրռիւ էր գրնում,
էնտեղ էր քու հէրն իր աղօթքն անում:
Քու հէրը մեռաւ, Աստուած խրռովեց,
Մրսրայ թագաւոր զօրքեր ժողովեց,
Մեր վանքն էլ եկաւ քանդեց էն սարում,
Բայց դեռ սեղանից լույս է բարձրանում...

XII

Դալիթը էս էլ երբ որ իմացաւ,
— Անն՛ի̲շ հորեղբայր, հորեղբա՛յր, ասաւ,
Որբ եմ ու անտէր աշխարքի վրրա,
Հէր չունեմ՝ դու ինձ հէրութիւն արա՛:
Էլ չեմ իջնի ես Մարութայ սարից,
Մինչեւ չրշինեմ մեր վանքր նորից:
Քեզանից կ՛ուզեմ հինգ հարիւր վարպետ,
Հինգ հազար բանւոր մրշակ նրրանց հետ,
Որ զամն՛ էս շաբաթ կանգնեն ու բանեն,
Առաջւան կարգով մեր վանքր շինեն:
    Գրնաց Օհանր ու բերաւ իր հետ
Հինգ հազար բանւոր, հինգ հարիւր վարպետ:
Վարպետ ու բանւոր եկան կանգնեցին,
Չրրր՛խկ հա թրրր՛խկ, նորից շինեցին,
Առաջւան կարգով, փառքով փառաւոր
Բարձր Մարութայ վանքր Տիրամօր:
Յրրւած միաբանք ետ նորից եկան,
Նորից թրնդացին աղօթք, շարական.
Ու երբ շէն արաւ հոր վանքր նորից,
Յած իջաւ Դալիթ Մարութայ սարից:

XIII

Համբաւը տարան Սրսրայ Մելիքին.
— Հապա՜ չես ասիլ՝ Դաւիթը կըրկին
Հոր վանքը շինել, իշխան է դատել,
Դու օխտը տարուան խարջը չես առել:
    Մելիք զայրացաւ.
— Գընացէ՛ք, ասաւ,
Բաղին, Կոզբաղին,
Սիւղին, Զարխաղին,
Սասմայ քար ու հող տակն ու վեր արէք,
Իմ օխտը տարուան խարաջը բերէք:
Քառսուն կոյս աղջիկ բերէք արմաղան,
Քառսուն կարճ կրնիկ, որ երկանք աղան,
Քառսունն էլ երկար, որ ուղտեր բառնան,
Իմ տանն ու դրան դարաւաշ դառնան:
    Ու Կոզբաղին առաւ զօրքեր.
— Գըլխի՛ս վըրայ, ասաւ, իմ տէր.
Գընամ հիմի քանդեմ Սասուն,
Կանայք բերեմ քառսուն-քառսուն,
Քառսուն բեռնով դեղին ոսկի,
Տեղը չրնչեմ հայոց ազգի:
    Ասաւ, Սրսրայ աղջիկ ու կին
Պար բռնեցին ու երգեցին.
— Մեր Կոզբաղին գընաց Սասուն,
Կանայք բերի քառսուն-քառսուն,
Քառսուն բեռնով ոսկի բերի,
Մեր ճակատին շարան շարի,
Կարմիր կովեր բերի կըթան՝
Գառնան շինենք եղ ու չորթան:

58

Ջա՛ն Կոզբադին, քաջ Կոզբադին,
Սասմայ Դաւթին զարկեց գետին:
    Ու Կոզբադին փրքւած, ունած,
— Շնորհակալ եմ, քոյրէ՛ր, գոռաց,
Մինչեւ գալըս դեռ համբերէք,
Էն ժամանակ պիտի պարէք . . .

XIV

        Էապէս երգով,
        Զոռով-զոռքով
Գոռ Կոզբադին մրտաւ Սասուն.
Օհան լրսեց՝ կապլեց լեզուն:
        Աղ ու հացով,
        Լաց ու թացով
        Առաջն ելաւ,
        Խրնդիրք արաւ.
— Ինչ որ կ՚ուզես՝ ա՛ռ, տա՛ր, ամա՛ն.
Վարդ աղջիկներ, կանայք Սասման,
Դառը դաղած դեղին ոսկին,
Միայն թէ զրթա մեր խեղճ ազգին,
Մի՛ կոտորիր, մի՛ տար մահու,
Վերեւ՝ Աստուած, ներքեւը՝ դու . . .
    Ասաւ, բերաւ, շարան-շարան
Վարդ աղջիկներ, կանայք Սասման:
Ու Կոզբադին կանգնեց, ջոկեց,
Մարագն արաւ, դուռը փակեց,
Քառսուն կույս աղջիկ, սիրուն, արմաղան,
Քառսուն կարճ կրնիկ, որ երկանք աղան,

Քառսունն էլ երկար, որ ուղտեր բաննան,
Մրսրայ Մելիքին ղարաւաշ դաննան:
Դէզ-դէզ կիտեց ղեղին ոսկին.
Սեւ սուգ կալաւ հայոց ազգին:

XV

Հէ՛յ, ո՞ւր ես, Դաւի՛թ, հայոց պահապան,
Քարը պատրուի — դուրս արի մէյդան:
Քանդած հոր վանքը որ շինեց նորից,
Յած իջաւ Դաւիթ Մարութայ սարից,
Ժանգոտած, անկոթ մի շեղբիկ գրտաւ,
Գրնաց՝ պառաւի շաղգամը մրտաւ.
Պառաւն էր. եկաւ՝ անէ՛ծք, աղաղա՛կ.
— Վա՛յ, խելա՛ռ Դաւիթ, շաղգամի տեղակ
Դու կըրակ ունես, ցաւ ունես, ասաւ,
Քու աչքն աշխարքում մենակ ի՞նձ տեսաւ.
Կորեկրս արիր գետնին հաւասար,
Էս էր մընացել ձրմեռուան պաշար,
Էս էլ կրտրում ես,
էլ ո՞նց ապրեմ ես:
Թէ կրտրիճ ես դու, ադեղդ ա՛ռ, գրնա՛,
Քու հոր աշխարքին տիրութիւն արա՛,
Քու հոր զանձր կե՛ր,
Թողել ես անտէր,
Մրսրայ թագաւոր ղըրկել է՜ տանի:
— Էլ ի՞նչ ես վրրէս բարկանում, նանի՛.
Էղ ի՞նչ ես ասում, ես չեմ հասկանում,
Մրսրայ թագաւոր մեր ի՞նչն է տանում:

60

Մրսրայ թագաւոր քու աչքն է հանում,
Դանդալoշ Դաւիթ. որդկել է հրրէն,
Եկել են Սասմայ քաղաքի վրրէն
Բաղին, Կոզբաղին,
Սիւդին, Չարխադին,
Թալան են տալի բովանդակ Սասում.
Քառունն բեռ ոսկի խառաջ են ուզում,
Քառունն կույս աղջիկ սիրուն, արմաղան,
Քառունն կարճ կրնիկ, որ երկանք աղան,
Քառունն էլ երկար, որ ուղտեր բանման,
Մրսրայ Մելիքին դարաւաշ դառնան:
— Ի՞նչ ես, ա՛յ պառաւ, էլ ինձ անիծում.
Ցոյց տուր մի տեսնեմ — ո՞րտեղ են ուզում:
— Ո՛րտեղ են ուզն՛ւմ... Մահրս տանի քե՛զ.
Դո՛ւ պէտք է էն հոր զաւակը լինէ՛ս ...
Եկել ես՝ էստեղ շաղգամ ես լափում ...
Ոսկին՝ Կոզբաղին ձեր տանն է չափում,
Աղջիկներ վիրլեկ մարագն են լցրած:
    Շաղգամը թողեց Դաւիթն ու գրնաց:
Տեսաւ՝ Կոզբաղին իրենց տան միջին
Չափում է ոսկին թեղած առաջին,
Սիւդին, Չարխադին պարկերն են բրռնել,
Չէնով Օհանն էլ շրլինքը ծրռել,
Կանգնել է հեռու, ձեռները ծոցին:
Տեսաւ, աչքերը արնով լրցուեցին:
— Վե՛ր կաց, Կոզբաղին, հեռո՛ւ կանգնիր դու,
Իմ հոր ոսկին է — ես եմ չափելու:
— Կոզբաղին ասաւ. — Է՛յ, Չէնով Օհան,
Կրտաս — տո՛ւր խարջր էս օխտր տարուան,
Թէ չէ՛ կր գրնամ, միրուքրս վրկայ,

Մբսրայ-Մելիքին կը պատմեմ, կը գայ,
Ձեր Սասմայ երկիր քար ու քանդ կ'անի,
Տեղը կը վարի, բոստան կը ցանի:
— Կորէ՛ք, անգգամ դուք Մբսրայ շըներ,
Բա չ°էք իմացել դուք Սասմայ ծըռեր ...
Մեռա՞ծ էք կարծում դուք մեզ, թէ° շրւաք,
Կ'ուզէք մեր երկիր դրնէք խարջի տա՛կ ...
      Բարկացաւ Դաւիթ, չափը շրւպրրտեց,
Տրւաւ Կոզբադնի գրլուխը չարդեց,
Ձափի վրշրանքը պատն անցաւ, գրնաց,
Մինչեւ օրս էլ դեռ գրնում է թրռած:
Ու էլաւ՝ թափած ոսկին թողեցին,
Հայոց աշխարքից փախան գրնացին
Բադին, Կոզբադին,
Սիւդին, Ձարխադին:

XVI

— Վա՛յ, վա՛յ, հորեղբա՛յր, ի՞նչ ասեմ ես քեզ.
Մենք ունենք էստեղ դեղին ոսկու դէզ,
Դու արել ես ինձ քաղաքի ծառան,
Դու թողել ես ինձ օտարի որրան ...
      Հորեղբայրն ասաւ. — Ա՛յ խենթ, խելւագար,
Ոսկին պահել եմ Մելիքի համար,
Որ քաղցըր լինի աչքը մեզ վրրայ:
Ձրտրւիր, հիմի որ զօրք առնի՛ գայ,
Սասմայ քար ու հող հեղեղի, տանի,
Ո°վ դէմը կ'երթայ, ո°վ կրռիւ կանի:

62

— Դու կա՛ց, հորեղբա՛յր, թող գայ, ե՛ս կ՚երթամ,
Կ՚երթամ, ե՛ս նրրան պատասխան կը տամ:
     Ու մութ մարագի դրռանը զարկեց,
Փակած աղջիկներ հանեց, արձակեց:
— Գրնացէ՛ք, ասաւ, ազատ ապրեցէ՛ք,
Սասունցի Դաւթին արեւ խրնդրեցէ՛ք:

XVII

Էսպէս չարդուած, արիւնլրւայ
Փախան, ընկան հողը Մրսրայ
Բաղին, Կոզբաղին,
Սիւդին, Չարխադին:
Մրսրայ կանայք հետւից տեսան,
Հետւից տեսան, ուրախացան
Ու ծափ տրւին կրտերներին.
— Եկա՛ն, եկա՛ն, բերի՛ն, բերի՛ն ...
          Մեր Կոզբադին գնաց Սասուն,
     Կանայք բերաւ քառսուն-քառսուն,
     Կարմիր կովեր բերաւ կրթան՝
          Գառնան շինենք եղ ու չորթան ...
Հէնց մօտեցան, նրկատեցին,
Ծափ ու խրնդում ընդհատեցին,
Քրրքրջացին
Ու կանչեցին.
— Է՛յ, Կոզբադին մեծաբերան,
Էղ ո՞րտեղից լերան-լերան,
Լերան-լերան կը գաս փախած,
Հաստ գրլուխրդ կիսից ճրդած:

63

Էն դո՞ւ չասիր՝ գրնամ Սասուն,
Կանայբ բերեմ քառսուն-քառսուն,
Քառսուն բեռնով ոսկի հանեմ,
Հայոց երկիր աւեր անեմ:
Գացիր Սասուն քանց զէլ զազան,
Եւ եւ զալի քանց շուն վազան ...
    Ու Կոզբադին խիստ բարկացաւ.
— Սո՛ւս կացէք դուք, լրրբե՛ր, ասաւ.
Ջեր մարդիկն էք տեսել դուք դեռ,
Դուք չէք տեսել Սասմայ ծռներ:
Սասմայ ծռներ լերան-լերան,
Նետեր ունեն մի-մի գերան.
Սասմայ երկիր քար ու կապան,
Դրժար սարեր, ձոր ու ծապան.
Նրրանց խոտեր — ինչպէս կեռ թուր,
Ջորբ չարդեցին երեք հարիւր ...
    Ասաւ ու էլ չառաւ դաղար,
Վրրազ-վրրազ, գրլխապատատ
Վազեց իրեն թագաւորին.
Խրնդաց թագուորն իր ապողին:
— Ապրէ՛ս, ապրէ՛ս, քաջ Կոզբադին,
Արժէ՛ կախեմ եւ քու ճրտին
Մեր դուգղունի մեծ նրշանը
Պարգեւ քու մեծ յաղթութեանը:
Ո՞ւր են, հապա առաջու բեր
Սասմայ ոսկին ու աղչիկներ:
    Ասաւ Մելիք, ու Կոզբադին
Գրլուխս տրւաւ մինչեւ գետին.
— Ապրա՞ծ կենաս, մեծ թագուոր,
Ջոռով փախայ եւ ձիաւոր,

Ո՞նց բերէի Սասմայ ոսկին:
Մի խենթ ծռնեց հայոց ազգին,
Ոչ ահ գիտի, ոչ տէր ու մեծ,
Գրլուխս էապէս տրւաւ ջարդեց.
«Չե՛մ տալ, ասաւ, իմ հօր ոսկին:
Չե՛մ տալ կանայքն իմ հայ ազգին,
Սասմայ երկիր ձեզ տեղ չրկայ ...
Քու թագաւոր, ասաւ, թո՛դ գայ,
Թող գայ՝ ինձ հետ կռիւ անի,
Թէ դոչաղ է՝ զղօղով տանի»:
      Կատաղեց, փրրփրեց Մրսրայ թագաւոր.
— Կանչեցէ՛ք, ասաւ, իմ զօրքը բոլոր.
Հազար հազար մարդ նորելուկ մանուկ,
Հազար հազար մարդ անբեխ, անմօրուք,
Հազար հազար մարդ բեխը նոր ծրլած,
Հազար հազար մարդ նոր թախտից ելած,
Հազար հազար մարդ թուխս միրուքաւոր,
Հազար հազար մարդ սպիտակ ալեւոր,
Հազար հազար մարդ, որ փողեր հրնչեն,
Հազար հազար մարդ, որ թրմբուկ զարկեն ...
Կանչեցէ՛ք, թող գան, հագնեն զէ՛նք, զրրա՛հ,
Կռիւ տի գրնամ ես Դաւթի վրրա,
Սասունն աւերեմ,
Հեղեղեմ, բերեմ:

XVIII

Էսպէս անհամար զօրքեր հաւաքեց,
Եկաւ Սասմայ դաշտ, բանակը զարկեց
Ու ծանրը նստեց Մսրայ թագաւոր:
Էնքան ահագին բազմութիւնն էն որ
Բաթմանայ չորին եկաւ ու չոքեց,
Ով եկաւ, խրմեց — գետը ցամաքեց.
Սասմայ քաղաքում մրնացին ծարաւ:
Չէնով Օհանին զարմանքը տարաւ:
Քուրքը ուսն առաւ, սարը բարձրացաւ.
Սարը բարձրացաւ, տեսաւ, ի՞նչ տեսաւ:
Ճերմակ վրրանից դաշտը ճերմակել,
Ասես՝ էն գիշեր ձրմեռը եկել,
Սպիտակ ձիւնով պատել էր Սասուն:
Լեղին չուր կտրեց, կապ ընկաւ լեզուն,
Հարա՛յ կանչելով փախաւ, տուն ընկաւ.
— Վա՛յ, փախէ՛ք, եկա՛ւ ... հա՛յ, հարա՛յ, եկաւ ...
— Ի՞նչը, հօրեղբա՛յր, ի՞նչը, ի՞նչն եկաւ ...
— Յաւն ու կրրակը Դաւթի պինչն եկաւ:
Մսրայ թագաւոր եղել է, եկել,
Եկել, մեր դաշտին բանակ է զարկել.
Թիւ կայ աստղերին, թիւ չկայ զօրքին ...
Վա՛յ մեր արեւին, վա՛յ մեր աշխարքին ...
Ե՛կ, ոսկին տանենք, աղջիկներ տանենք,
Չոքենք առաջին, պաղատանք անենք,
Գուցէ թէ զրթայ,
Մեզ սրրի չրտայ ...
— Դու կա՛ց, հօրեղբայր, դու դարդ մի՛ անիր.
Գրնա՛, քու օղում դու հանգիստ քրնիր.

66

Հիմի ես կելնեմ, Սասմայ դաշտ կ'երթամ.
Մըսրա-Մելիքին պատասխան կը տամ:
    Ու գրնաց Դավիթ ծանօթ պառաւին.
— Նանի ջա՛ն, ասաւ, ժանգոտած ու հին
Երկաթի կրտոր, անթարոց, շամփուր,
Ինչ ունես չունես՝ հաւաքի՛ր, ինձ տուր,
Մի էշ էլ գրտիր, որ վրրէն նրստեմ,
Կրռիւ տի գրնամ Մրսրայ զօրքի դեմ:
— Վա՛յ, Դալի՛թ, ասաւ, մահս տանի քեզ.
Դո՞ւ պէտք է էն հօր զաւակը լինե՞ս ...
Քու հէրն ունէր կրռիւ համար
Հրրեղէն ձի, ոսկի քամար,
Ծալ-ծալ կապէն, գուռզը պողպատ,
Թամբ սադափէն, կուռ սադաւարտ,
Խաշ պատրաս}in իր աջ բազկին,
Զրրահ շապիկ, Թուր Կեծակին,
Դու եկել ես, ա՛յ խենթ ու ծուռ,
Ինձնից կ'ուզես էշ ու շամփո՞ւր ...
— Ամա՛ն, նանի՛, չեմ լրսել դեռ:
Ո՞ւր են հիմի իմ հօր զէնքեր:
— Հօրեղբօրրդ գրնա հարցուր.
Ո՞ւր են, ասա, հանի՛ր, բեր, տուր:
Բան է, թէ որ չրտայ սիրով,
Աչքը հանի՛ր, խրլիր զօրով:

XIX

Դալիթ գրնաց հորեղբոր մօտ.
— Է՜յ հորեղբայր, կանչեց հեռսու,
Իմ հէրն ունէր կրուի համար
Հրրեղէն ձի, ուկի քամար,
Ծալ-ծալ կապէն, գուզգը պողպատ,
Թամբ սադափէն, կուռ սադաւարտ,
Խաչ պատրասուին իր աջ բազկին
Զրրահ շապիկ, Թուր Կեծակին,
Կր տաս — բեր տուր...
— Վա՜յ, Դալիթ ջա՜ն,
Աhից գոռաց Զէնով Օhան.
Քու hոր մաhուան տարուց — օրից
Դուրս չեմ hանել ձին ախոռից,
Ոչ սրնդուկից Թուր-Կայծակին,
Զրրահ շապիկ, ուկի գոտին...
Ինձ թող, ամա՜ն, մի՛ սպանիր,
Կ'ուզես — hրրէն, գրնա hանի՛ր:

XX

Հազաւ Դալիթ զէնք ու զրրահ,
Կապեց գոտին, Թուր-Կեծակին,
Խաչն էլ իր յաղթ բազկի վրրա,
Ելաւ, hեծաւ Առhիծ hոր ձին,
Հոր ձին hեծաւ ու մրտրակեց.
Զէնով Օhան լալով երգեց.

68

— Ափսո՜ս, հազա՜ր ափսոս հրրեղէն մեր ձին,
        Ա՜խ, հրրեղէն մեր ձին.
Ափսո՜ս, հազա՜ր ափսոս մեր ոսկի զօտին,
        Ա՜խ, մեր ոսկի զօտին.
Ափսո՜ս, թանկ կապէն, որ հազին տարալ,
        Ա՜խ, որ հազին տարալ . . .
    Դալիթ բարկացալ,
    Ձին քըրշեց, դարձալ,
    Օհանը վախեց,
    Իր երգը փոխեց.
«Ափսո՜ս, նորելուկ Դալիթըս կորալ,
        Ա՜խ, Դալիթըս կորալ:»
        Էս որ իմացալ,
Դալիթ մեղմացալ,
Իջալ, Օհանի ձեռքը համբուրեց:
Զէնով Օհանն էլ, ինչպես հայր ու մեծ,
Օրհնեց, խրրատեց նրրան հայրաբար,
Դէպի Սասմայ դաշտ ղրրալ ճանապարհի:

<h2 style="text-align:center">XXI</h2>

    Սասունցի Դաւթին ունէր մի քեռի.
Անունը Թօրոս, ահեղ աժդահա:
Սա էլ իմացալ համբաւը կըրռի,
Մի բարդի ուսին զալիս է ահա:
Գալիս է հեռուից բարձրը զոռալով.
— Ի՜նչ էք վեր եկել էս դաշտի միջում,
Քանի զրլխանի մարդիկ էք կամ ո՞վ,
Սասունցի Դաւթին որ չէք ճանաչում . . .

Բա չե՞ք իմանում, որ էստեղ է նա
Գալու՝ խաղացնի իր ձին թեւաւոր,
Զրկեցե՞ք, հիմի ուր որ է՝ կը գայ,
Եկել եմ սրրբեմ մեյդանը էսոր:

Ասաւ ու քաշեց իր ուսի բարդին,
Սրրբեց բանակից մի քրսան վրրան . . .
Դաւիթն էլ ահա սարի գագաթին
Կանգնած՝ գոռում է վիշապի նրման.

— Ով քրնած էք՝ արթուն կացե՞ք,
Ով արթուն էք՝ եւլե՞ք, կեցե՞ք.
Ով կեցել էք՝ զենք կապեցե՞ք,
Զե՞նք էք կապել՝ ձի թամբեցե՞ք,
Զի էք թամբել՝ եւլե՞ք, հեծե՞ք.
Յետոյ չասե՞ք, թէ մենք քրնած —
Դաւիթ գող-գող եկաւ, գրնաց . . .

Էսպես կանչեց, ասպանդակեց,
Ու, ինչ ամպից կեծակ զարկի,
Մրսրայ գործքի մեջտեղ զարկեց,
Շողացնելով Թուր-Կայծակին:

Զարդեց, փրրշեց մինչեւ կեսոր.
Կեսոր արինն եւաւ հեղեղ,
Քրշեց, տարաւ հագարաւոր
Մարդ ու դիակ ողջ միատեղ:

Կար գործքի մեջ մի աւեւոր,
Աշխարք տեսած ու բանագետ.

— Տրդե՛րք, ասա, ճամբայ տրո՛ւէք,
Գ՛նամ խօսեմ ես Դալթի հետ:

Գ՛նաց, կանգնեց Դալթի առաջ,
Էսպէս խօսեց էն ծերունին.
— Դալար կենա՛, կուրդդ, ո՛վ քաջ,
Սուրրդ կրտրուկ միշտ քու ձեռին:

Մի ծերունու խօսքին մրտիկ,
Տե՛ս, քու խելքը ինչ է կրտրում:
Ի՞նչ են արել քեզ էս մարդիկ,
Հէ՞ր ես սրրանց դու կոտորում:

Ամէն մինը մի մօր որդի,
Ամէն մինը մի տան ճրրագ,
Որը կինն է թողել էնտեղ
Աչքը ճամբին, խեղճ ու կրրակ,

Որը մի տուն լիք մանուկներ,
Որը ծրնող աղքատ ու ծեր,
Որը լացով, քողն երեսին
Նորապսակ ջահել հարսին . . .

Թագաւորը զօռով-թրրով
Հաւաքել է, էստեղ բերել:
Խեղճ մարդիկ ենք՝ պակաս օրով,
Մենք քեզ վրնաս ի՞նչ ենք արել:

Թագաւորն է քու թշնամին,
Կրծիւ ունես — իր հետ արա,

Հէ՞ր ես քաշում Թուր-Կայծակին
Էս անճարակ խալխի վրրա:

— Լավ ես ասում դու, ծերունի՛,
Ասավ Դավիթն ալևորին,
Բայց թագավորն ո՞ւր է հիմի,
Որ սեւ կապեմ նրրա օրին:

— Մեծ վրրանում քրնած է նա,
Է՛ն, որ միջից ծուխը կելնի.
Էն ծուխն էլ հո ծուխս չի որ կայ,
Գոլորշին է իր բերանի:

Ասին. դէպի մեծ վրրանը
Ասպանդակեց Դավիթն իր ձին,
Քըշեց, զրնաց ու դրռանը
Գոռաց կանգնած արաբներին.

— Ո՞ւր է, ասա, ի՞նչ է կորել,
Դուրս կանչեցէ՛ք, զալ ասպարեզ,
Թէ մահ չունի՛ մահ եմ բերել,
Գըրող չունի՛ գըրողն եմ ես . . .

— Մելիքն, ասին, քուն է մրտել,
Օխտր օրով պետք է քրնի.
Երեք օրն է դեռ անցկացել,
Չորս օր էլ կա, քունը առնի:

— Ի՞նչ, բերել է ազքատ ու խեղճ
Խալխին լըցրել ծովն արիւնի,

Ինքը մրտել վրրանի մէջ՝
Օխտը օրով հանգիստ քրնի՛...

Քրնել-մրնել չեմ հասկանում,
Վե՛ր կացրէք շո՛ւտ, դուրս գայ մէյդան,
Էնպէս դրրան ես քրնացնեմ,
Որ չը զարթնի էլ յաւիտեան:

— Ելան մարդիկ ճարահատուած
Շամփուր դրրին թէժ կրրակին
Ու զարկեցին խոր մրրափած
Մրսրայ-Մելքի բաց կրրնկին:

— Օ՛ֆ, էլ հանգիստ քուն չունի մարդ
Էս անիծուած լրլի ձեռից,
Խոր մրրռնցաց հրսկան հանդարտ
Ու շուտ եկալ, քրնեց նորից:

Ելան, բերին մեծ գութանի
Խոփը՝ դրրին թէժ կրրակին,
Ու կաս-կարմիր, կեծկրծալի,
Շիկնած տրրին մերկ թիկունքին:

— Օ՛ֆ, էլ հանգիստ քուն չունի մարդ
Էս անիրաւ մօձակներից.
Աչքը բացաւ հրսկան հանդարտ,
Ուզում էր էտ քրնել նորից,

Տեսաւ՝ Դաւթին: Գլուխն ահեղ
Վեր բարձրացրեց մրռրնչալով,

Փրչեց վրրէն, որ թրոցրնի
Էն ադրրհին մի փրչելով:

Տեսաւ, տեղից ժամ չի գալի,
Զարմանքն ու աh պատեց հոգին:
Արնոտ աչքերն րսպաննալի
Յառեց խոժոռ Դաւթի աչքին:

Նայեց թէ չէ, զգաց՝ իր մէջ
Տաար գոմշի ուժ պակասեց:
Պառկած տեղից վրա նստեց
Ու ժպտալով հետո խոսեց.

— Բարով, Դաւի՛թ, հոգնած ես դեռ.
Ե՛կ, մի նստի՛ր, խոսենք կարգին,
Յետոյ դարձեալ կռիւ կանենք,
Եթէ կռիւ կ՚ուզես կրրկին ...

Իր վրրանում բրնակալը
Քառսուն գազ խոր հոր էր փորել,
Յանցով փակել մուտ բերանը,
Վրրէն փափուկ խալի փռրել:

Ում որ յաղթել չէր կարենում,
Շողոմելով կանչում էր նա,
Նրստեցնում էր իր վրրանում
Էն կորստեան հորի վրրա:

Իջալ Դաւիթ ձիուցը ցած,
Գրնաց, նրստեց ... րնկաւ հորը:

— Հա՛, հա՛, հա՛, հա՛, քահ-քահ խրնդաց
Մրսրայ դաժան թագաւորը:

— Դէ, թող հիմի գրնա՝ խաւար
Հորում փրթի, էնքան մրնայ:
Ու ահագին մի ջաղացքար
Բերաւ, դրրաւ հորի վրրա:

XXII

Քրնեց էն գիշեր Չէնով Օհանը:
Գիշերն երազում երեւաց ծերին՝
Մրսրայ երկրնքում արեւ ճառագած,
Սեւ ամպ էր պատել Սասմայ սարերին:

Սաստիկ վախեցած վեր թրրաւ տեղից:
— Վա՛յ, կրնի՛կ, ասաւ, մի ճրրագ արա՛,
Գրնա՞ց մեր անփորձ Դաւիթը ձեռից,
Սեւ ամպ էր իջել Սասունի վրրա:

— Հողե՞մ գրլուխդ, ասաւ կրնիկը,
Ո՞վ գիտի՝ Դաւիթն ո՛ւր է քէֆ անում ...
Դու էլ քեզ համար քու տանը րնկած՝
Ուրիշի համար երազ ես տեսնում:

Քրնեց Օհանը: Վեր կացաւ դարձեալ.
— Կրնի՛կ, Դաւիթը նեղ տեղն է րնկած.
Մրսրայ վառ աստղը շողում էր պայծառ,
Մեր աստղը հիւանդ ցոլքում դալկացած:

— Ի՞նչ եղաւ քեզ, մա՛րդ, գիշերուան կիսին.
Բարկացաւ վրրէն կրնիկն աղմուկով:
Խաչ քաշեց էլ ետ Օհանն երեսին,
Շուն եկաւ, քրնեց խրոռված հոգով:

Մի ուրիշ պատկեր աւելի ահեղ
Տեսաւ՝ երկրնքի բարձր կամարում
Վառւում էր Մրարայ աստղը փառահեղ,
Սաամայ աստղիկը սուգւեց խաւարում:

Ջարթնեց վախեցած: — Տունդ քանդուի, կի՞ն,
Ես ո՞նց լրսեցի քու էդ կարճ խելքին.
Կորաւ մեն-մենակ մեր ջահիլն անտէր.
Վե՛ր կաց, շ'ւտ արա, զէնքերրս մի բե՛ր ...

XXIII

Ելաւ Օհան, գումր մրտաւ,
Ջարկեց ձերմակ ձիու մէջքի՛ն.
— Է՛յ, ձերմակ ձի, մինչ է՞րբ, ասաւ,
Կր հասցրնես Դաւթի կրրւին:

«Մինչեւ լուսր կր հասցնեմ».
Ու ձին տրւաւ փորր գետին.
— Մէ՛ջքդ կոտրի, լուսն ի՞նչ անեմ.
Լաշի՞ն հասնեմ ես թէ՞ նաշին:

Կարմիր ձիու մէջքին զարկեց.
Սա էլ երետ փորր գետին.

— Զա՛ն կարմիր ծի, մին՞ չ է՞րբ դու ինձ
Կը հասցընես Դաւթի կրուին:

«Մի՛ ժամի մէջ, կարմիրն ասալ,
Կը հասցընեմ Դաւթի կրուին»:
— Լեղի դառնայ, սեւ մահ ու ցաւ,
Ինչ տրուել եմ քեզ՝ էն գարին:

Հերթը եկաւ սեւին հասաւ
Գետին չերեւ փորը սեւ ծին:
— Է՜յ, ջան Սեւուկ, մին՞ չ է՞րբ, ասաւ,
Կը հասցընես Դաւթի կրուին:

«Եթէ ամուր մէջքիս մրնաս,
Ոտրդ դրնես ասպանդակին,
Մին՞ չեւ մէկել ոտրդ շուռ տաս,
Կը հասցընեմ», ասաւ սեւ ծին:

XXIV

Սեւ ծին քաշեց Ջէնով Օհան,
Զախը դրրաւ ասպանդակին,
Աջն էլ մինչեւ շուռ տար վրրան,
Կանգնեց Սասմայ սարի գլխին:

Տեսաւ՝ Դաւթի նրժոյգն անտեր
Սարերն ընկած խրրխրնջալով,
Ներքեւ Մրսրայ գործք չոբաձ,
Ինչպէս անծեր ծրփուն մի ծով:

77

Օխտը գումշի կաշի հագաւ,
Որ չպատռի իրեն զօրից,
Կանգնեց Օհան, ամպի նման
Գոռաց Սասմայ սարի ծերից:

— Հէ՛յ-հէ՛յ Դալի՛թ, ո՛րտեղ ես դու.
Յիշի՛ր խաչը քո աջ թեւի,
Սուրբ Տիրամօր անունը տո՛ւր,
Ու դուրս արի լոյսն արեւի ...

Չէնը գրնաց, դրմբրմբալով՝
Դալթի ականջն ընկաւ հորում.
— Հա՛յ-հա՛յ, ասաւ, հորեղբայրս է,
Սասմայ սարից ի՞նձ է գոռում:

Ո՛վ Մարութայ Աստուածածին,
Ո՛վ անմահ խաչ պատարագի,
Զէ՛զ եմ կանչել, — հասէ՛ք Դալթին ...
Կանչեց, տեղից ելաւ որթի,

Էնպէս զարկեց չադացքարին՝
Քարը եղաւ հազար կրտոր,
Կրտորները երկինք թռան,
Ու գնում են մինչեւ խսոր:

Ելաւ հորից, կանգնեց ահեղ,
Սարսափի կալաւ դեւ Մելիքին:
— Դալիթ ախպէր, ե՛կ դեռ խստեղ,
Սեղան նրստե՛նք, խոսենք կարգի՛ն ...

— Էլ չեմ նրստիլ ես քու հագին,
Դու տրմարդի, վախկոտ ու նենգ.
Շո՛ւտ, գէնքրդ առ, հեծիր քու ձին,
Դո՛ւրս եկ մէյդան, կռիւ անենք:

— Կռիւ անենք, ասաւ Մելիք,
Իմն է միայն զարկն առաջին:
— Քոնն է, զարկի՛ր, կանչեց Դաւիթ,
Գրնաց, կեցաւ դաշտի միջին:

Ելաւ, կանգնեց Մսրայ-Մելիք,
Իր գուրգն առաւ, հեծաւ իր ձին,
Քրշեց, գրնաց մինչ Դիարբէքիր
Ու էնտեղից եկաւ կրրկին:

Երեք հազար լիդր էր քաշում
Հրսկայական իր մրկունդը.
Եկաւ, զարկեց. կորաւ փոշում
Ու երերաց երկրի գունդը:

— Երկիր քանդուեց կամ ժաժք եղաւ,
Ասին մարդիկ շատ աշխարքում:
— Չէ՛, ասացին, արևի ծարա
Հրսկաներն են իրար զարկում: ´

— Մեռաւ Դաւիթ էս մի զարկից,
Ասաւ Մելիք իրեն զօրքին:
— Կենդանի է՛մ, ամպի տակից
Գոռաց Դաւիթ Մսրայ-Մելքին:

— Հա՛յ-հա՛յ, մօտիկ տեղից եկայ,
Տե՛ս, ո՞րտեղից հիմի կը գամ:
Ու վերկացաւ, կանգնեց հրական,
Իր ձին հեծաւ երկրորդ անգամ:

Երկրորդ անգամ քրշեց Հալաբ
Ու բաց թողեց ձին Հալաբից.
Բուք վեր կացաւ, տեղ ու տարափ,
Արար աշխարհ դողաց թափից:

Եկաւ, զարկեց. զարկի ձէնից
Մօտիկ մարդիկ ողջ խրլացան:
— Գրնա՛ց Դալիթ Սասմայ տանից,
Գուժեց զոռոզ Մըսրայ արքան:

— Կենդանի՛ եմ, կանչեց Դալիթ,
Մի՛ն էլ արի՛ — հերքն ինձ հասաւ:
— Հա՛յ-հա՛յ, մօտիկ տեղից եկայ,
Կանչեց Մելիք ու վերկացաւ:

Երրորդ անգամ հեծաւ իր ձին,
Գրնաց մինչեւ հողը Մըսրայ,
Ու էնտեղից, գուրգը ձեռին
Քըշեց, եկաւ Դաւթի վրրա:

Եկաւ, զարկեց բոլոր ուժով,
Ծանըր զարկով հրակայական,
Փոշին էլաւ Սասմայ դաշտից,
Բրրնեց երեսն արեգական:

Երեք գիշեր ու երեք օր
Փոշին կանգնեց ամպի նման,
Երեք գիշեր ու երեք օր
Բոթը տրւին Դալթի մահուան։

Երբ որ անցաւ երեք օրը,
Էն ամպի պէս կանգնած փոշում
Կանգնեց Դալիթ, ինչպէս սարը,
Գլրգուն սարը մէգ-մրշուշում։

— Մելի՛ք, ասաւ, ո՞ւմն է հերթը։
Սարսափի կալաւ զոռ Մելիքին,
Մահուան դողը ընկաւ սիրտը
Ու տապ առաւ գռռող հոգին։

Գռնաց, խորունկ մի հոր փորեց,
Իջաւ, մրտաւ վիհն էն խաւար,
Վրրէն քաշեց քառսուն կաշի
Ու քառասուն ջաղացի քար։

Մրոռընչալով ելաւ տեղից
Էն առիւծի առիւծ որդին,
Իր ճին հեծաւ ու փոթորկեց,
Խաղաց, շողաց Թուր-Կայծակին։

Առաջ վազեց մազերն արձակ
Մելքի պառաւ մայրը ջաղու։
— Դալի՛թ, մազրս ա՛ն ոտիդ տակ,
Էդ մի զարկը ի՛նձ քաշխիր դու։

Երկրորդ անգամ թուրը քաշեց.
Էս անգամ էլ եկավ թուրը.
— Դալի՛թ, եթէ կ'ուզես, կանչեց,
Իմ սրրտին զա՛րկ երկրորդ թուրը . . .

Վերջին զարկի ժամը հասավ,
Ելավ Դալիթ երրորդ անգամ.
— Էս մի զարկն ու Աստուած, ասավ,
Էլ մարդ չրգայ, պէտք է որ տամ:

Ասավ, ելավ ու փոթորկեց,
Թրռավ, ցոլաց Դալթի հուր ճին,
Ճին փոթորկեց, փայլատակեց
Ու գած իջավ Թուր-Կայծակին:

Անցավ քառսուն գոմշի կաշին,
Անցավ քառսուն քարերը գած,
Միջից կրտրեց ժանտ հրրէշին,
Օխտը զազ էլ դէնը գրնաց:

— Կենդանի՛ եմ, մին էլ արի՛,
Գոռաց Մելիք հորի տակից:
Դալիթ լրսեց, շատ զարմացաւ
Իրեն զարկից, Թուր-Կայծակից . . .

— Մելի՛ք, ասավ, թա'փի տուր մի քեզ:
Ու թափի տրւավ Մելիքն իրեն,
Միջից եղավ ճիշտ երկու կէս,
Մէկն ընկավ դէսն ու մ
իւսը՝ դէն:

Էս որ տեսաւ Սրսրայ բանակ,
Ջուր կրտրրւեց ահ ու վախից:
Դալիթ կանչեց. — Մի՛ վախենաք,
Ակա՜նջ արէք հալա դեռ ինձ:

Դուք ըրանչպար մարդիկ, ասաւ,
Ջուրկ ու խաւար, քաղցած ու մերկ,
Հազար ու մի կրրակ ու ցաւ,
Հազար ու մի հոգսեր ունէք:

Ի՞նչ էք առել նետ ու աղեղ,
Եկել թափել օտար դաշտեր.
Չէ՞ որ մենք էլ ունենք տուն-տեղ,
Մենք էլ ունենք մանուկ ու ծեր ...

Զանձրացե՞լ էք խաղաղ ու հաշտ
Հողագործի օր ու կեանքից,
Թէ՞ զրգւել էք ձեր հանդ ու դաշտ,
Ձեր հունձ ու փունջ, վար ու ցանքից ...

Դարձէ՛ք եկած ճանապարհով
Ձեր հայրենի հողը Սրսրայ.
Բայց թէ մին էլ գէնք ու զօռով
Վեր էք կացել դուք մեզ վրրայ,

Հորում լինեն քառսուն գազ խոր
Թէ ջաղացի քարի տակին, —
Կ'ելնեն ձեր դէմ, ինչպէս այսօր,
Սասմայ Դալիթ, Թուր-Կայծակին:

Էն ժամանակ Աստուած գիտի,
Ով մեզանից կըլնի փոշման.
Մե՞նք, որ կելնենք ահեղ մարտի,
Թէ դուք, որ մեզ արիք դուշման ...

SOPHENE